11-2 $5.00

HOLDUP ON
BOOTJACK HILL

TO JOHN HENRY MADDOX IV

*Whose great-great-grandmother told
me about the rope swing and the
Candle Man, and whose great-grand-
mother Sally could have been Callie
herself.*

Books by Marion Garthwaite

COARSE GOLD GULCH

MARIO

MYSTERY OF SKULL CAP ISLAND

HOLDUP ON BOOTJACK HILL

Marion Garthwaite

HOLDUP ON
BOOTJACK HILL

Illustrated by
LEO SUMMERS

DOUBLEDAY & COMPANY, INC.
GARDEN CITY, NEW YORK

ACKNOWLEDGMENTS

I would like to thank JACK AND JILL MAGA-
ZINE for permission to use the material in
this story already published under the same
title.

Reprinted by special permission from JACK AND JILL
© 1959 The Curtis Publishing Company

TABLE OF CONTENTS

I THE MORNING OF
THE HOLDUP

Everybody in the small California town of Hardpan
believed that the holdup on Bootjack Hill was not
a girl's business. That is, everybody but Callie herself. Callie believed the holdup was everybody's
business, because it meant deep trouble for Callie's
Indian friends, old Tansy Loosefoot and her son
Winky.

Hardpan was a cluster of brick and wooden build-
ings scattered along Sawmill Creek. By 1862 most
of the free gold in this part of California had been
dug and spent. Men had turned to farming and

lumbering when the pick-and-shovel gold was gone.

Along Sawmill Creek there were rotting remnants of old mining cradles, with here and there the heavy stones of a rock crusher. Old flumes, both the wooden troughs and the dug ditches, still laced the town with swift-flowing waters.

Many of the Hardpan families had bought land from the Indians who were left. Newcomers like Mr. Hoag, who kept the store, and his partner Jim Turnbeck took what land they wanted and drove off the Indians.

Down the creek from the stage road was the one-room schoolhouse that became a church whenever any kind of parson who could preach the word of God came to town. Last year a scholarly man named Timothy Patch had come to Hardpan. He had been talked into staying on, by the Deans and Jensens, to teach school on week days and to preach the Gospel on Sundays.

Timothy Patch was a quiet-spoken man for the most part, but he stood for no nonsense at school and backed it up with cane and ruler. On Sundays he tackled sin and the Devil with what Callie's pa called "the full-bodied howl of a bull-roarer."

The day the stage was stopped, and a lone bandit made off with the gold and Mr. Patch's watch, was the last day of school. It was also the day that ended in disgrace for Callie, both at home and at school. Part of it was her own fault, like being late, but Callie blamed most of it on that Andy Jensen.

Andy was the only pupil Callie's age in the school. She had been pleased when the Jensens moved to Hardpan, and she would have liked being friends with Andy. But Andy made it plain, right from the start, that he had no use for girls.

The whole school knew there was war to the tooth between Anders Jensen and California Dean.

Callie had lived all of her eleven years in Hardpan. She had been born during the first hard winter after the family had come to California by wagon train. It was Pa, delighted to have a girl-child after three strapping boys, who named her.

"It's all right to call the boys after the apostles," Pa said. "The handle on a boy needs to be stout. But anything as pretty as this young 'un should have a name to match. We'll call her California."

The day before the stage was robbed, Pa and Callie's three older brothers—Matthew, Mark, and Luke—had gone over to Cedar Brook for a week of felling trees. Callie was left at home with Ma and Sma' John, aged two. Chances were, Callie always felt, if Pa had been home he would have straightened things out before Callie got herself mixed up in the holdup. With Pa gone, it was Callie—and Andy, she had to admit grudgingly—who plunged into the grim business of trying to save Winky Loosefoot.

When Callie looked down from her attic window early that morning and saw the calf in with the cow, she knew that the milking was done. That meant she'd be late for school if she didn't step lively.

9

Then she would have to stay in at noon. She didn't want that to happen the last day of school. Mr. Patch was a stickler for being on time.

Also, she admitted to herself, she didn't want to give Andy Jensen that much satisfaction.

Callie lifted her best blue calico dress from behind the curtain that made her clothes closet. She slid the dress over her head, fumbling with the tiny buttons down the front. The skirt was heavy with rows of braid stitched on by hand to cover the lines where Ma had let out tucks.

"I wish I'd stop growing forevermore higher," groaned Callie, "and get a little wider."

She could just hear Andy Jensen's taunts, "Tall and lean, cross and mean, who is? who is? Bean Pole Dean!" Callie's eyes were nearly black with anger when she thought of it.

When Andy made up something like that, all the boys in school took it up. They could see it made Callie mad. She wrinkled up her nose. "Thinks he's so smart!" she muttered. She'd show that Andy.

She stooped down to get her best shoes from behind the curtain. These were red buttoned boots that old Peter Shoemaker had brought her for a gift last fall when he came to Hardpan to make shoes for all the children.

The red boots were Callie's pride and joy. Old Peter had made them of red leather as soft as kid gloves, with fat little red-leather tassels that bobbed with every step that Callie took.

She had to pull and tug to get them on because

her feet had been growing along with the rest of her.

"Cal-lee!" Ma called from the kitchen.

"Coming, Ma," shouted Callie.

It took some time to coax the little red-glass buttons into the stitched buttonholes with Ma's long silver buttonhook.

Callie stared at the brown face in the wavery mirror on her wall while she undid her long braids. It should have been a pleasant face looking back at her, with blue eyes black-lashed, high color in her cheeks, and a wide and generous mouth. But through some flaw the mirror made her face thinner and longer than it was and one eye higher than the other. If she moved a little, her forehead bulged or her chin disappeared, until even the dimple just below the corner of her mouth failed to show how merry her face could be.

It was bad enough to be the only girl in the family, she was thinking, with the three older boys big enough to go off with Pa. It was even worse with only two girls in the one-room school—and Sue Ellen Binks three years younger than Callie. Sue Ellen was small and pudgy and pretty much of a tattletale.

"Cal-lee!" There was no mistaking the impatience in Ma's voice.

Callie thumped down the steep steps from the attic into the warm kitchen that smelled of salt rising bread and the sweetness of two-year-old Sma' John, fresh scrubbed.

Callie sat down to sour-cream hotcakes and fresh milk still warm from the milking.

Ma had lifted the hatch in the floor to haul up over a pulley a heavy crock from the icy water of the flume that raced below the kitchen floor. She took out the butter, close-wrapped in a damp, linen napkin, and lifted a pitcher of clotted cream to the table, where Callie was drowning her hotcakes in elderberry syrup.

"It's lonesome around here without Pa and the boys," complained Callie.

Ma nodded as she lowered the hatch over the yawning hole in the floor. "Get right along, Callie, or you're going to be late. Finish buttering this bread while I comb out your hair."

Callie smoothed the soft butter on two thick slices of bread and spread one side with the shining purple of wild grape jelly. She winced as her mother pulled her hair into smooth, skin-tight braids.

"Eee-yow! Ma! You're braiding my eyebrows in with it!"

Ma laughed as she pulled some long strands of hair from the brush to twist around the end of the braid. "You've lost every last ribbon you have!" Ma's voice was impatient. "Hold still, Callie. You jump around like a cricket."

Callie wrapped the thick sandwich in a fringed napkin and stuffed it into the covered pail she used for lunches. She cut a huge slab of gingerbread to put in her pocket for that empty feeling at recess.

She patted Sma' John on his fat little rear with

one hand and scooped up her book with the other. This was one of the few textbooks in the schoolhouse. It had been well used by Matthew, Mark, and Luke before Callie came along. The outside had been carefully sewn into a linen cover, but the inside was in shreds.

Ma's kiss landed on Callie's nose as she opened the door and clattered down the steps. She went down through the dew-wet garden in ten jumps and across the wooden bridge over the flume in two, her tassels flying.

Beyond the Jensen place Callie could see the old Indian woman, Tansy Loosefoot, plodding along behind her son Winky, as was proper for an Indian squaw.

"Hey, wait!" yelled Callie. She set out on a dead run to catch up with Tansy.

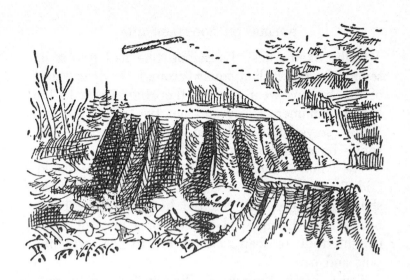

II TANSY AND WINKY

The old Indian woman swung slowly around to face
Callie. Her coarse gray hair hung about her face in
straggling wisps, almost hiding her bloodshot eyes.
Her face was a mass of wrinkles. She wore a finely
woven basket cap on her head to protect her forehead from the rubbing of the string strap that
reached to a back cradle of woven reeds high up
on her shoulder blades.

Tansy was bent over with the weight of the sleeping baby strapped in the cradle, his black-thatched
head bobbing like a sycamore ball. Beside the baby,
Tansy was carrying a basket of camas bulbs balanced
on one hip.

Callie liked Tansy Loosefoot. She had grown up seeing the old Indian squaw around Hardpan. Most of the Indians went up into the High Sierra in the heat of summer. Tansy and her two sons Tom and Winky stayed late and came back early, when the snows began to block the trails.

The younger Indians found what work they could. Old Tansy appeared at Callie's back door whenever she was hungry, and Ma fed her. In return Tansy brought the Deans wild berries, or a mess of fresh-caught trout, or soap root for Ma to use scrubbing pots and pans.

Tansy often brought Callie shelled piñon nuts wrapped in a dirty square of calico. They were sweet and meaty little nuts, and Callie shared them with Sma' John who loved them as much as she did. She always put them in two piles on the kitchen table, counting out, "One-for-you-and-one-for-me," with Sma' John's blue eyes sparkling with pleasure just above the table top.

Winky had often worked for Pa before the boys got so big. He taught the Dean boys how to track game and where to find the best fish. He told Callie where good arrowheads could be found on the fringes of an old Indian battleground above the abandoned sawmill and down the creek below the covered bridge where the Indians had camped by the stream to make arrowheads of the black volcanic glass they packed back from the mountains. One Easter morning Winky had given Callie an obsidian skinning knife as broad as her hand—a knife that was the envy of every boy in Hardpan. It had been chipped as cunningly as a jewel, sharp and rough along the edges, evenly shaped and balanced.

Pa said the Indians hadn't been given a fair chance when the miners took over the rivers and streams in the mining country to dig for gold.

Many of the Indians had retreated to the mountains. The stubborn ones like Tansy and her two sons Tom and Winky clung to their makeshift huts on lands the Indians had called their own since time began. Now men like Mr. Hoag and Jim Turnbeck wanted these lands for their own use, to run cattle or to cut lumber. They made no offers for these lands. They just took them.

The Indians could never understand how strangers like Mr. Hoag and Jim Turnbeck could show them a paper that took their lands away from them. Pa and the Jensens and most of the old-timers stuck up for the Indians. They said that the Indian camps, where the grinding rocks were worn into deep holes from centuries of use, belonged to the Indians, papers or no papers.

Callie knew that Jim Turnbeck had taken Winky's land around Cold Spring. He had driven Winky's stock so far away that Winky had not been able to track down all of his cattle.

Everybody in town knew about this. Most of the old-timers meant to do something about it, but none of them did. Pa meant to take it up with Jim Turnbeck, but the packer spent most of his time on the road hauling supplies for the store. It was hard for anyone as busy as Pa to lay hands on a man who was here today and gone tomorrow. Pa forgot about Winky and Cold Spring when the chance came, sooner than he expected, to cut the trees at Cedar Brook. He and the boys had gone off to the lumbering camp, leaving Winky to cope with Jim Turnbeck as best he could.

Callie skidded to a stop in front of the old Indian squaw. "Hello, Tansy!" she gulped, out of breath.

Tansy beamed at Callie, her face crinkled with pleasure. "'Allo!" Her voice was so low it was almost a whisper. She shifted the heavy basket of bulbs to the other hip.

Callie dug down in her pocket. "Look, Tansy." Callie was never sure how much Tansy could understand, so her own voice was loud and hearty. "Here's a piece of gingerbread for you. M-m-mmm, good!" She pinched off a corner of the brown square, put it in her own mouth, and rolled her eyes. "Honest, Tansy, it's real good."

She broke the slab of gingerbread in two and offered the larger piece to Tansy.

Tansy set her bulb basket down on a stump. She reached for the piece of gingerbread Callie held out and bit off a big chunk with her toothless gums. Tansy seemed surprised at first at the spicy taste. Then she smacked her lips loudly.

She chewed off another bite and rolled the rest into a tight ball. She pulled the papoose basket over her shoulder and pushed the thick brown wad of dough into the roof of the baby's mouth.

The baby went on sleeping and nodding, sucking at the gingerbread and smiling in his sleep.

Callie grinned. "Just hope gingerbread's good for babies," she said cheerfully.

Tansy nodded.

"Your baby, Tansy?"

Tansy laughed and shook her head. "Na. Winky's baby."

"Well, you tell Winky's squaw she ought to carry him herself. He's getting too heavy for Grandma to lug around."

"Hu!" Tansy hooted, as she stooped to lift the heavy basket of bulbs.

Callie loped on down the road. "Hello, Winky!" she called out as she caught up with Tansy's son.

Winky's grin was friendly. He was a tall Indian with a fringed jacket stretched taut over broad shoulders and too short in the sleeves for his long, brown arms. He wore a brightly patterned calico rag around his head to keep his black hair out of his eyes. His trousers were a pair of Pa's old Sunday britches, frayed and patched with doeskin. His bare feet were caked with dried mud.

Callie hauled the last of the gingerbread from her pocket. "Here, Winky, might as well finish it up." She dusted crumbs off her hands, while Winky bit into the gingerbread. He chewed solemnly and Callie watched him with satisfaction.

"Your pa want Winky to work?" he asked.

"Not right now, Winky. He's over at Cedar Brook

cutting trees. He'll be home in a week. Come see him next week, huh?"

"No work." Winky spread his hands and shrugged. "No work, no eat."

Callie felt bad about this. "You go tell Ma. Maybe she'll have something for you to do. She can always find plenty to keep *me* busy."

Tansy caught up with them. She pointed at Callie's red button boots. "Muy pretty! Pretty!"

Callie kicked her foot out to show how the tassels bobbed. "Can't wear them much longer. Pa says what a pity I have such a good understanding. I'd save them for you, Tansy, if I thought you could get into them."

"Hu!" Tansy put her own foot out beside Callie's. Her shabby doeskin moccasin was scuffed and muddy, the heel of it rolled down in a wad under her foot. The moccasin was bound to her bare ankle with a rawhide thong. On the toe of it a few broken pink and black porcupine quills still clung, showing where a pattern had once been stitched.

The old woman's foot and moccasin made two of Callie's trim red boots, and Callie's gay laugh rang out.

Tansy laughed, too. Then Winky joined in. They stood there, the three of them, laughing like fools, while a meadow lark sang from a tree stump and a dove mourned sadly from a thicket.

All about them was the warm sweet dusty smell of summer. On the bank above the stream the last of the wild iris bloomed in the forest litter. Mountain lilac was a blue drift on the dryer slopes, and mariposa lilies swayed on long stems in the sunny spots. It was a day for laughter, a day to be alive.

The faint clamor of the brass bell rang out from the schoolhouse down the road.

"Eee-yow!" yelled Callie. "That means I'm late!"

She waved a long arm at Winky and Tansy as she bolted off down the hill.

III DISGRACE AT SCHOOL

Mr. Patch had stopped ringing the bell by the time
Callie reached the schoolhouse. The schoolmaster's
face was unlined and kindly until his righteous wrath
was kindled—as it was now. A network of tiny veins
over his cheekbones gave him a high color, and he
always looked freshly scrubbed. His clothes were
brushed and threadbare, his linen white but frayed.
A rebellious lock of hair strayed down over his forehead. He impatiently tossed it back.

Callie thought that Mr. Patch knew more than anyone in the world. Not only about God and the Devil,
which she would expect of a preacher. Mr. Patch
knew about gods and goddesses, rocks and stars, and

the names of all the flowers in the hills, even those tucked away in the fern thickets along the streams, though these were seldom the common names that Callie knew.

Callie liked Mr. Patch and she hadn't meant to disappoint him by being tardy.

He put the big bell on the floor by the door, folded his arms and raised his eyebrows. Callie stood in the doorway, gasping from her sprint down the hill.

"Well, California," he said, "you run true to form when you can manage to be late on the last day of school." He shook his head in tight-lipped exasperation. "You will have to stay in at noon."

Callie nodded unhappily. She had no breath left.

Under the stern eye of Mr. Patch, Callie kept her seat at noon when the rest of the children filed to the door and then spilled out into the sunshine with shouts and whoops.

"Tsk! Tsk! Tsk!" Andy Jensen was saying as he left the room. "A diller, a dollar, what makes you come *so late?*"

Callie ignored him. She ate her sandwich as slowly as possible, listening to the shouts outside. The schoolhouse seemed hot and stuffy even with the door and window open. The desks were drab and shabby, unpainted and marred, since pine is a soft wood and tempting to a jackknife.

On a low one-step platform at the front of the room was an unvarnished table that stood for the master's desk. Beside it was a leather globe, long since pressed into flat planes over a base of wire. The leather was so old and dark and cracked it was hard to tell the oceans from the land. The few textbooks, owned by the children, were stacked on one side of the table, with cane and ruler beside them.

Callie yawned and moved over to the window. Andy and the older boys were out of sight, down by the creek. Sue Ellen sat by herself under an oak tree, chewing her way through a big lunch.

At the end of half an hour Mr. Patch came back to the schoolroom, patting his forehead with his folded handkerchief. "That sun has a bite to it, California," he was saying. "I feel like Icarus himself, with his wax melting."

From his vest pocket he pulled a fat watch and opened the front of it. He held it to his ear with a gentle smile of satisfaction. He rubbed his handkerchief around the face of the watch, and pried open its thin gold back, looking for any speck of dust.

"What are all those wheels for, Mr. Patch?"

He held the watch closer so she could see it better. "Those are the works of the timepiece, California. That's what it takes to tell time. Each of those wheels is set upon a tiny jewel hard enough to stand that continual motion."

"My goodness!" Callie was impressed.

"A machine like this is a monument to man's ingenuity," Mr. Patch went on. "This watch not only tells the time of day. It tells the day of the week and the month of the year."

"Why, that's magic!" It almost made Callie dizzy to see all those little wheels spinning so busily.

Mr. Patch beamed at her. "It would seem so. It was my grandfather's watch. His name was the same as mine. The initials engraved on the cover stand for Timothy Castlewood Patch. He willed me the watch. I prize it very highly."

He snapped the lid shut and tucked the watch away in his vest pocket. He reached for the hand bell.

The children, still shouting, came chasing over to the door. They settled down to filing past the schoolmaster in seemly fashion.

"Our water supply is low, Anders," Mr. Patch told Andy. "You and William have my permission to go to the well in the Hoag yard for a fresh supply."

Andy picked up the nearly empty bucket and a stick to thrust through the handle. He grinned at Willie Binks. It was a coveted privilege to go for water. It meant being out-of-doors and out of school that much longer.

It was adding insult to injury for Callie after being inside all the noon recess. Mr. Patch, Callie remembered, had never sent the girls for water, probably because he thought a full bucket of water was too heavy. Callie felt that was silly. She could carry any load Andy Jensen could carry. She had to admit to herself it would be a lopsided journey with tall, rangy Callie on one side of the stick and short, pudgy Sue Ellen on the other. But she thought it wasn't fair.

She was still cross about it when the boys came

back, especially since she had read the caustic comment Mr. Patch had written in the copybook he handed back to her.

Andy swung the bucket away from Willie when they reached the door, carrying it singlehanded across the room to the up-ended keg by the window. He took down the tin dipper hanging above the bucket and helped himself to the first drink.

Everybody in the room used the same dipper, but it was an unwritten law that any water left in the dipper after a drink must be thrown out.

Andy finished his drink. He ignored the open window. He had one eye on Mr. Patch handing out copybooks and the other on Sue Ellen Binks. She would tell on him if she saw what he had in mind.

Andy waited until Mr. Patch reached Sue Ellen's desk. A quick toss sloshed the half dipperful of water over Callie's red boots.

Callie watched the leather turn wet and dark, her lips set tight. She glared at Andy as he walked back to the seat they shared together. He was looking at the ceiling and pretending to whistle.

Sue Ellen didn't have to share a desk with a boy, Callie thought angrily. She hated sitting next to that Andy Jensen. But it was the only desk large enough for either one of them, so she had to make the best of it.

The afternoon was given over to recitations. Andy reeled off twenty lines from the *Iliad* without a break. He made faces at Callie behind Mr. Patch's back, and Callie stumbled over her lines about "the

quality of mercy" from *The Merchant of Venice.*
Andy was holding his nose when she took her seat.

Callie turned her back on him. She sat with her
feet out in the aisle, as far away from Andy as she
could get.

"Sit up straight, California," ordered Mr. Patch.
"Feet front."

Callie flounced around. One black pigtail slapped
wetly between her shoulder blades. It had been
dipped in Callie's own ink bottle. She knew there
must be ink all over the back of her best dress. There
were snorts and snickers from some of the boys.

In a blaze of fury Callie whirled around and
slapped Andy's face with a resounding smack.

There was an appalled silence.

"California!"

Andy's gray eyes were smarting with tears, but he
was grinning at the dire sound in Mr. Patch's voice.

"Come up to the front of the room, California
Dean," ordered Mr. Patch.

Callie got slowly to her feet, looking at the heavy
ruler in his hand with eyes that were sick with shame
and misery.

Hardly a week went by that didn't find a luckless
boy being smacked with the ruler or being caned.
Mr. Patch didn't believe in sparing the rod. He laid
it on with a right good will. The little boys cried,
the big boys grinned and grunted, while Callie and
Sue Ellen squirmed. So far the master had never pun-
ished the girls, except with extra work or staying
after school.

Callie wished she had remembered that it was the last day of school. She wished she could have waited just one more day. She would have had all summer to get even with Andy.

"Can you give me any sensible reason why a young lady should strike a young gentleman in a classroom?" thundered Mr. Patch when Callie stood facing him on the platform.

"No, sir." Callie tried to keep the quaver out of her voice.

"Put your hand out, California."

She stood the pain of the slashing blows without flinching, until her hands were blistered.

"You will sit on the stool in the corner for the rest of the afternoon," said Mr. Patch.

This, Callie felt, was worse than the licking. The stool was high and hard. The rungs of it were too far down for even Callie's long legs to reach. The red button boots dangled and swung, while the edge of the stool bit into the back of her knees. The afternoon seemed to drag on forever.

The voices of the children droned on. Callie saw Andy's gray eyes laughing at her, his teeth caught over his lower lip. She sat up straight on the stool, her jaw set. She kept her eyes on a knot in the rough lumber wall.

She'd never speak to that Andy Jensen again as long as she lived. She'd never have a thing to do with him. And one of these days she'd show that Andy.

The school day finally ended and the rest of the

children filed out. Callie climbed stiffly down from the high stool.

Mr. Patch picked up a worn carpetbag. "Well, California, this is hail and farewell for the summer." He seemed to have forgotten her sins and their punishment. "I do not feel that you are one of my more conspicuous successes of the year. I may have taught you a few facts. Almost anyone can learn facts. The only point in learning them is that somewhere along the line you also learn to think."

"Yes, sir." Callie stood on one foot and then the other. She was opening and shutting her blistered hands to see how much they hurt.

"I doubt very much," Mr. Patch went on, packing the last of his papers in his bag, "if you have done much thinking to date. You are a creature of instinct, California. When you are angry you lash out. You want what you want and you take it. The world is full of takers, California, and so few givers." He peered at her over his spectacles.

"Yes, sir."

Mr. Patch laughed at the blank look on Callie's face. "Have a good summer, California," he said briskly.

"Thank you, Mr. Patch. I hope you do, too."

He carried his bag outside, locking the school door behind him. "It will be a change, certainly. I am going to work in the woods, for a lumber camp. Not the cutting and hauling, mind you. I would never be the man for that. They need help with sums and figures. A timekeeper they call it. And speaking of time——" He pulled out his gold watch. "I must be on time to catch the stage."

He patted the watch gently and slid it back in his vest pocket.

IV   MR. HOAG AND THE
PEPPERMINT STICK

Callie walked down to the stable where Mr. Patch
had joined a small group of people waiting for the
stage. She wished that she dared wait for the stage
herself. There was something very exciting about the
big stagecoaches as they came rumbling and rocking and wheeling in, with the dust in choking clouds
behind them, the driver fingering the long ribbons
of reins with one hand and blowing his horn with the
other.

Callie liked to think of the stages coming all the
way down from the northern mines on the weekly

trip to Sacramento. She tried to picture herself sitting inside the swaying coach, with the driver cracking his whip overhead. Beneath his seat would be the gold shipment from the mines, smelted down into small, heavy cones and packed in a stout express box. Callie's feet slowed to a drag as she thought of it. The stage was one of the few contacts Hardpan had with the outside world. It brought news and mail and sometimes even a visitor. It was one of Callie's dearest daydreams to picture herself riding off some fine day in the swaying coach, like Cinderella going to the Ball.

In her mind's eye she could see the stage swaying and creaking, the six horses covered with lather as they slowed down for the stop at the Hardpan stable. Waiting for them, hatted and gloved, beneath a ruffled pink parasol, would be Miss California Dean, as pretty as any picture in *Graham's Magazine*.

She would be wearing a pink ruffled dress, her raven locks piled high under a scrap of pink hat. Over her arm she carried Ma's black bag embroidered with blue forget-me-nots.

No one could keep his eyes off this beautiful girl. A dozen men leapt forward to hand her into the coach. And Mr. Patch just stood there, unable to believe that this exquisite creature could possibly be his erstwhile pupil who came late to school and slapped people's faces.

The driver would shout at the horses. "Tan-tan-ta-ra," the horn would sing. Then off they would dash, the red dust rolling, the wheels spinning, leaving the bystanders behind them in the small town of Hardpan sighing with envy. They would go thundering through the covered bridge and around the lower slopes of Bootjack Mountain, slowing to a walk as they climbed up the steep hill into the larger settlement of Bootjack. In Bootjack, Callie took time out from her dream to remember, there was a church, sixteen saloons and a separate store for ladies clothes known as an Emporium.

Callie reached the stable as the coach in her dream slowed to a crawl for the long pull. She knew that her mother would not like to have her hanging around the stable waiting for the stagecoach. Ma would say it was no place for a girl.

Callie scuffed her feet in the dust. She was hoping the stage would come jingling down the road before her feet had carried her past. If she were waiting to take it, where would she be going? It didn't matter. To the river first. Callie had never been to the river. Then maybe down the river road to Sacramento. Or even just around the mountain to Bootjack. It didn't matter at all. Just to be going was good enough.

Callie had never been on a stage. She'd never been farther away from home than Bootjack, where Pa had taken her one never-to-be-forgotten day in a spring wagon. She had seen the church with its tall steeple, the saloons with their swinging doors and the Ladies' Emporium, all in one gulp.

She sighed. I'll be old and gray and tottering, she was thinking, before anything more than that ever happens to me.

35

She could see Mr. Hoag peering over the lanterns and gold pans and bolts of calico in his store window across the narrow street. He didn't seem to be watching the road for the stage. He was looking up toward the Bootjack trail, squinting his eyes against the sun. Callie looked up that way, too. She could see as far as the fork in the trail where Tom and Winky Loosefoot, old Tansy's sons, were talking together. Tom started off through the pines for Custer Creek. Winky took the right-hand trail that went straight over the shoulder of the mountain into Bootjack.

Callie turned back to find Mr. Hoag leaning over the heaped-up gear, tapping on the window. Callie didn't like Mr. Hoag, but when he beckoned to her she crossed the street and walked in the door of the store.

I'll ask for mail, she decided, making her way around the cracker barrel and the pickle crock and the potbellied stove. Maybe the stage would be in by then.

The store was so full of food and clothing and hardware there were only narrow runways in which to get about. The light from the small and dusty windows was blocked by clothes hanging from the rafters and boxes piled on the floor.

Callie stumbled over a cluster of milk buckets. She barked her elbow on the corner of a case of buttons and notions.

Mr. Hoag pushed his way over to her through dangling underwear and overalls. He was a loose-

jointed man with a two days' growth of gray beard
bristling along his jawbone. There were sticky stains
in the deep creases below his lips and spots on his
vest. The sleeves of his shirt were bloused up over
elastic bands, and his pants were bloused over the
tops of his heavy boots.

Bunched in the left-hand pocket of his vest were
half a dozen red and white peppermint sticks. He
held one of them between his lips like a cigar, and
he had sucked it white.

"Thought I'd see if we had any mail, Mr. Hoag,"
said Callie brightly. Her mouth watered as she
sniffed the delicious spiciness of peppermint. "With
the boys and Pa away from home——"

"No, y'aint. Your pa ain't been gone long enough.
Now there might come some mail on this stage due
in. You want to wait?" He turned the peppermint
stick between his lips and wiped his sticky fingers
on his vest.

"No, I guess not."

Mr. Hoag reached into his vest pocket and drew
out a stick of candy. He offered it to Callie.

"I haven't any money," she said, backing off.

"My compliments."

"Thank you!" Callie was thinking, as she took the
candy, that it wasn't a bit like Mr. Hoag to be so
generous. She had never known him to give away the
peppermint sticks he carried around with him. His
store smelled of stale crackers, and salt fish, and
dress goods. But Mr. Hoag himself always smelled
of peppermint.

"I saw you looking up the hill a bit ago," Mr. Hoag was saying as he rolled up a length of calico. "Seen the same thing I did, I betcha. I sent Winky on an errand, but you seen those two no-count Loosefoot boys up there on the hill with their heads together, talking secrets. An' then Winky taking off over the Bootjack trail. Do you know you can beat the stage to Bootjack over that hill, if you're spry? You know that?"

Callie nodded. Andy had done it last year. His mother, on her way to Sacramento, had left her spectacles on Mr. Hoag's counter. The stage had been gone ten minutes when Andy had seen the glasses. He had put them in his pocket and set out up the trail at a steady lope. The foot trail across the mountain was several miles shorter than the stage road, which must follow Sawmill Creek around the lower edges of Bootjack Mountain, and then climb the steep slope out of it. Andy had caught the stage and handed over the glasses with no trouble at all.

"Just you remember you saw them Indians on that trail," Mr. Hoag was saying.

Callie wandered out, sucking the candy. She stood on the porch that shaded the store from the hot afternoon sun. She could see Mr. Patch and several others still waiting for the stage. There was no telling when it would be in.

Callie walked along to the blacksmith shop and turned up the road toward home. The flume she walked along was more like a creek than a man-made ditch. Ferns and briars grew along the banks, and tiny, bell-like flowers were rooted in the rocks. The sun dappled the clear running water, and the alders overhead hung listless in the heat.

Callie was thinking of Andy. She would have been glad to be friends with someone her own age. But Andy was a tease, a practical joker. When he began playing tricks on her, Callie felt she had to pay him back. It had gone from bad to worse, until now they were sworn enemies.

Callie thought of the water on her boots, and the ink on her best dress. She thought of her disgrace at school, and how her hands stung. She remembered how Andy had called her, just yesterday, "Dean, Dean, the long String Bean!"

She snapped off a piece of candy and chewed it, her eyes half closed. She meant to get even with that Andy, if it took all summer.

"Just you wait, Andy Jensen!" she gritted between her teeth. "Just you wait!"

V DISGRACE AT HOME

Beyond the blacksmith shop, Callie could see Willie and Sue Ellen Binks walking along the flume beneath the sycamores. She ran to catch up as soon as she saw that Andy wasn't with them. "Where's Andy?" she demanded.

"He said he had to meet the stage."

"Mr. Patch was at the stable waiting, but I didn't see Andy."

"Most likely he's in the forge blowin' the bellows," answered Willie. "Carl Oats says Andy's real good at blowin' an' keepin' the fire hot."

"He's good at blowing his own horn, too," said Callie sourly.

Callie slowed down again after the other two
turned off up the hill. Just before she reached the
Jensen place, she crossed over below the old wooden
flume that early miners had built to carry water to
their mining cradles on Sawmill Creek. The timbers
that held it up leaned at crazy angles and where the
wood had warped and the water leaked, blackberries
and willows had sprung up in a tangle of whips and
thorns. In one cool muddy wallow three of the Jensen pigs were bedded deep in the mire. Such nice,
soft, black mud. Just right for mud balls.

Callie grinned. She crossed to the other side of the
Jensen gate, far enough away so she wouldn't dis-
turb the pigs. Callie had a great respect for aroused
pigs.

She chewed off two long willow shoots and peeled
them clean and slick. She gathered the mud into soft
round balls and stuck the balled mud on the tips of
the limber sticks. She crouched in the bushes, dipping her mud balls in and out of a puddle under the
flume to keep the mud from drying out.

She was well hidden from the road, but she had
a clear view of the Jensen gate. If she kept down
out of sight, Andy would never know for sure who
had mud balled him.

It was cool and green and smelled of mud and
mint in the bushes. Tiny gnats plagued her, and mos-
quitoes hummed and buzzed and bit. She hoped
Andy wouldn't take too long, and as she thought it
she heard him whistling on the road.

Through the heavy screen of branches Callie

watched him come over the bridge, loaded down with bundles. Callie ducked. She kept her head down until she heard him turn in toward his own gate. She rose silently. She watched him put down his bundles to open the gate. She whipped a long stick backwards, then forwards, and gave it a quick snap.

The soft mud ball caught Andy on his cheekbone, splattering the whole side of his face with mud. As he whirled about, half blinded, the second mud ball splotched over his shirt and coat.

Callie, down behind her screen of bushes, her head in her lap, was trying to smother her delighted laughter. Two bull's-eyes!

There were angry words out by the gate. Callie checked her laughter. It was not Andy who was scolding. It was Andy's mother.

"Ach!" wailed Mrs. Jensen. "All over mud you haff! Who iss it mean enough? See once now. Your clean shirt, fresh vashed und pressed. Your goot closes all over mud!"

Callie felt sick at heart. She hadn't thought of the trouble she'd make for Andy's mother. She hadn't seen Mrs. Jensen coming behind him. Andy must have met his mother at the stage, to bring her bundles home for her.

Callie stayed perfectly still until she heard the two of them go on up the path to the house, with Mrs. Jensen still wailing about the mud. She crept out of the bushes and ran the rest of the way home.

For the rest of the afternoon there was a lump of fear as big as a buckeye ball in Callie's chest. She

was nervous and fidgety. When a blue jay squawked outside the kitchen window, she dropped the turnip she was peeling. The round white ball bounced across the floor and rolled under the stove.

"Butterfingers!" scolded Ma.

Callie was setting the table for supper when she saw Mrs. Jensen, with Andy in tow, coming up the walk between the beds of violets. Andy was hanging back, looking far from happy. Mrs. Jensen pushed him up the steps, her face grim.

Callie crept into the kitchen. Her heart was pounding so hard her mother must surely hear it. There was a sharp knock at the front door.

"You go, Sma' John," said Callie. She wished there were some hole to crawl into, some good safe hiding place.

Sma' John trotted off.

"I come about dot bad girl," Mrs. Jensen was saying. "Dot Callie."

"Callie?" asked Ma. "Why?"

"Because she iss a limb of Satan, dot's vy! Mud she slings by my boy. All over his Sunday closes. See already." She turned Andy about and pointed to the splotches of half-dried mud. "De last day of school, so his best closes he puts on. Und now mud. So mean it iss. All over mud!"

"Aw! Ma!" said Andy squirming.

"Callie did that?" Ma's voice was shocked. "Are you sure it was Callie?"

"Certainly I'm sure. To all de houses I go. Sue

45

Ellen Binks, she says nobody can sling mud like Callie. Und all over his goot suit!"

"Callie!" There was a dreadful ring in the sound of it.

Callie came to the kitchen door. "Yes, ma'am," she said in a small voice.

"Did you throw mud at Andy?"

"Yes, ma'am."

"You go straight up to your room, California Dean. I'll attend to you later."

Callie marched over to the steep steps that led up to her attic room. Her head was high and her cheeks flushed. She wouldn't look at Mrs. Jensen or at Andy. I don't care, she told herself fiercely. Two bull's-eyes!

She took off her best dress and laid it across a chair. She could see the ink stains on the back of it. She unbuttoned her boots. The stain of the water Andy had thrown on them was long since dry, but they were muddy from the damp ground below the flume. She set them outside the curtain of her closet to be cleaned later. She was too sick at heart to do it now.

She crept in under the quilt of her bed and lay there listening. She heard the Jensens leave and her mother go back into the kitchen. I'm just good and thankful Pa isn't home, she was thinking. Pa whipped a lot harder than Ma ever did. But Ma always cried, and that made Callie feel worse than the switching.

She could hear Sma' John galloping around the

kitchen, and the thump of his wooden broomstick. Outside the hens were clucking sleepily as they settled up in the apple trees to roost.

She heard someone come to the back door. She could hear Ma's voice asking questions.

A few minutes later she heard her mother's footsteps on the attic stairs. Callie braced herself. She peered fearfully over the edge of the quilt and was surprised not to see a switch in her mother's hand.

She didn't want to ask the question, but the words popped out. "Aren't you going to whip me?"

Her mother sat down on the edge of the bed. "No, Callie, I'm not, though I make no doubt you deserve it. Andy came back. He told me about the ink, all over your good dress. He said you hadn't told on him at school, or at home either. He said you'd had one licking already today, and more his fault than yours."

"Can we get the ink out?" Callie was glad to change the subject.

Ma looked the dress over. "I'll put it to soak in some sour milk. That will take most of it out. You have nearly had the good of that dress."

"May I come downstairs?"

"No, Callie, you may not." Ma ran a work-worn hand over her own brown cheek. "And that's nowhere near enough to make you stop and think. My own daughter, and that hard-working woman with her boy all over mud!"

Callie stirred restlessly. "He can be ornery mean, Andy Jensen can."

"That's no excuse. You're too big now, Callie, for mudslinging and such. With Pa and the boys away from home, looks like you better settle down and act like a girl should."

Callie wished her mother would stop scolding and go back downstairs. The one sandwich she had eaten for lunch seemed days away. Callie knew she was going to be really hungry long before breakfast.

"Andy told me something else," Ma was saying. "The stage was held up this afternoon on the Bootjack Hill. Whoever it was took everybody's money and Mr. Patch's gold watch, as well as the express box full of gold.

Callie sat bolt upright. "Ma! When? Where? May I go down and find out about it? May I?"

"No, Callie, you're to stay in bed. Andy says people in town are saying that it was Winky Loosefoot who robbed the stage."

"Winky!" Callie's voice was indignant. "Why, of course he didn't! Why in the world would Winky want to rob the stage? That is just plain ridiculous!"

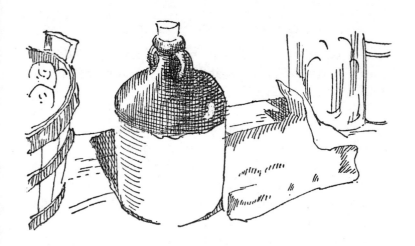

VI "STRING 'EM UP!
LIFT 'EM!"

Callie couldn't help being thankful, while she listened to the news, that her own small crimes would be swallowed up in this big one.

"What else did they say, Ma?"

"There was just one man. He wore a sack over his head, with eyeholes cut in it. He held up the stage on the steepest part of the Bootjack Hill. In broad daylight! Think of it! After he got the express box, he robbed the passengers. Mr. Patch is back in town feeling mighty sorry over losing his grandpa's watch."

"Oh, Ma! Mr. Patch set real store by that watch."

Callie could see the small wheels spinning and Mr. Patch patting the big watch gently before he slid it into his vest pocket.

"He doesn't want to go off to the lumber camp if there's any chance of getting it back," said Ma. "Andy says the men in town claim it was Winky."

Callie shook her head. "It couldn't be Winky." She was quite positive. "What could an Indian do with all that gold? The minute he tried to trade in a single cone of it, he'd get caught."

Suddenly Callie was seeing Mr. Hoag at the store as he peered up the mountain to where Tansy's two sons were talking together. She remembered how Winky had turned away on the trail that went over the hill to Bootjack. She could hear Mr. Hoag's whining voice, "You can beat the stage to Bootjack over that hill, if you're spry. You know that?"

Callie did know it. Andy had done it with no trouble at all. Suppose Mr. Hoag tried to make her tell that she had seen Winky and Tom up there on the Bootjack trail? Callie set her lips tight. Nobody could make Callie Dean tell anything if she didn't choose to. She certainly wasn't going to tell about Winky.

She was hearing Mr. Hoag's voice. "Just you remember you saw them Indians on that trail." Callie shivered.

"Mr. Hoag says," Ma went on, "that he's caught Winky being light-fingered in the store a time or two. The Jensens don't believe it. Andy says they've always found Winky honest."

"Well, I don't believe it, and Pa wouldn't either."

Callie didn't want to be on Andy's side for any reason, but she couldn't help it this time. "Winky's as honest as anybody. He could have stolen a lot of things around here if he had wanted to. He never took one thing."

After Ma had gone downstairs Callie undressed and climbed back into bed. Her blistered hands stung and burned. Hunger was an empty gnawing inside of her. Coyotes had set up a yapping chorus on the hill behind the house.

She heard Ma go out to see that the mother hen was tucked safely in her coop. An owl hooted softly, "Hoo-oo, hoo, hoo," in the locust tree beside Callie's window. It was a sad and lonely sound.

Ordinarily none of this could have kept her awake. It was the thought of the old Indian squaw that kept Callie tossing and turning. She liked old Tansy Loosefoot, and she didn't believe for one minute that either of Tansy's sons would rob the stage.

The next morning Callie went down to the store on an errand for her mother. She put her empty jug and four pats of butter on the counter. There were angry voices as the men milled around the hay rakes and kegs of nails. Andy was sitting on the end of the counter, munching a cracker from the cracker barrel.

"Here's Callie now," said Mr. Hoag. "She can tell you." He peered over his glasses at her and the jug and the pats of butter. His grizzled whiskers were another day older on his sticky chin. "First tell me what you come for, before you forget it."

"Ma needs a jug of molasses. I brought the jug and the butter to pay for it."

"We all know Winky done it," argued one of the men. "Them Loosefoots been asking for trouble, ever since Jim Turnbeck turned that outfit away from Cold Spring."

Callie whirled around, her eyes almost black. "The Indians have always had that spring," she said indignantly. "What justs and rights has Jim Turnbeck to run them off?"

"That's part of Jim's land, is why," answered Mr. Hoag. "Claimed and filed on." He poured the slow black gobs of molasses into a funnel he had stuck into the mouth of the brown jug. "Seems like none of us can turn around without these Indians git underfoot. Too lazy to work, so they just help theirselves."

"Makes sense to run 'em all out," said a man with a black spade beard.

"Start with Winky then."

"Run 'em out? Why not string 'em up?" demanded a red-shirted man.

"Lift 'em, that's what I say."

"Here's your 'lasses, Callie," said Mr. Hoag. He pushed the jug across the counter. "An' here's another peppermint stick. Now you just tell these men what you an' me saw yesterday. I sent Winky on an errand, but Callie an' me, we both saw Tom an' Winky Loosefoot up there on the hill, with their heads together. The stage wasn't even in yet, was it, Callie? An' Winky took off over the hill to Bootjack,

in plenty of time to catch the stage on that Bootjack Hill. Tell 'em, Callie."

Callie set her lips in a tight line. She wished she
could shout out, "I saw no such thing!" but she
couldn't. She picked up the heavy jug of molasses,
leaving the peppermint stick on the counter.

Mr. Hoag leaned over and plucked at her sleeve.
"Do as I say, Callie Dean," he insisted. "You tell us
how you an' me saw Winky head up that trail in
time to catch the stage."

Callie's face shut down tight. "You can't make
anybody into a thief"—she said between clenched
teeth—"Winky or anybody—just by saying so."

There was a muttering in the crowd. Andy slid
off the counter. He hooked his finger into the other
handle of the jug. "Come on, Bean Pole," he said,
"before you get into trouble." He pulled on his handle of the jug.

Callie couldn't get her finger out of her handle,
so she was forced to follow Andy out on the porch
of the store.

Once outside Andy reached into his pocket and
pulled out the peppermint stick. He broke it, measured the pieces, and handed Callie the shorter one.

Callie gave a yelp of fury. "He didn't give that
candy to you," she pointed out angrily.

"You wouldn't have had any of it, Miss High-and-
Mighty, if I hadn't picked it up."

They walked along under the locust trees, swinging the jug between them. "Do you think Winky did
it?" asked Callie.

"No. Do you?"

"Of course not." Callie's voice was scornful. "But how can we prove it? Men like that won't listen. They get all worked up until they're apt to go off half-cocked. How can we prove that Winky didn't do it?"

"I don't know. We'll have to do it pretty quick. They'll go after Winky and arrest him when they find him. They might even do worse—hang him even —the way they talk now."

"Does Tansy know?" asked Callie.

Andy shrugged. "It's hard to tell. I think they all know. There isn't an Indian in sight this morning."

"Maybe somebody ought to tell Tansy, just to make sure."

"Tansy and the rest of them are probably over at the Indian camporee on Custer Creek. Tansy might listen to you, if you went over there, Callie.

Callie had never been to the Indian camp. She was fairly sure that Ma would not let her go—certainly not alone. But Callie didn't want to go with Andy. The less she had to do with Andy Jensen the better.

"Maybe Ma might let me go for blackberries this afternoon. They're ripe enough for jelly, maybe even jam, on that cut-over hill above the sawmill. I might run into Tansy up there, or one of the other Indians. I could send her a message telling her to get Winky out of here."

Andy dropped his handle of the molasses jug. "If she says you can, I'll meet you at the upper bridge right after noon." He started off.

"I can go by myself," Callie called after him crossly.

"Bring pails and old gloves. The stickers are murder." He kept on going, leaving Callie to struggle with the heavy jug.

She was grateful to Andy for clearing out when she saw Willie and Sue Ellen Binks coming down the road. She'd hate to have any of the other children in town see her hauling a jug of molasses home with Andy Jensen. After all, she was thinking, they knew well enough that she and Andy were sworn enemies.

But were they? Yesterday they were. But today there were Tansy and Winky, an old Indian and her son, in trouble. And, like it or not, for the first time since Andy Jensen had come to Hardpan, Callie and Andy were hanging on to the same jug.

VII CALLIE AND
THE CANDLE MAN

Callie almost forgot about the blackberries when she came to the smithy and saw the painted wagon of Mr. Diamond, the candle man. Callie despised making candles. She was hoping with all her heart that Ma would let Mr. Diamond make up a winter's supply.

Mr. Diamond lived in his wagon. He traveled up and down the mountain settlements making candles.

His wagon was painted a bright blue. Against this background, in shining gold, were all kinds of lamps and candles—from the ancient oil lamps that the wise virgins might have used to the gilded sun itself rising in a burst of glory across the back doors. On both sides, in gilt letters, were the words FIAT LUX. Mr. Diamond had told Callie that they meant "Let there be light." The words were a little tarnished by rain and sun, but Callie thought that *Fiat Lux* was a fine motto for a man who made candles.

Mr. Diamond was a little man, neat and spry. His wagon was immaculate, and even the huge oxen that pulled it were well-brushed and clean. He hung the greasy tools of his trade—the molds and dippers, the bags of tallow, the balls of braided string for wicks— in swinging boxes below the wagon bed, out of sight and smell. His tiny built-in bed was made up with a bolster beneath a blue and white quilt. His small store of food was behind closed cupboard doors.

Callie could not imagine how he could work with hot grease and never get a spot on his sturdy, well-kept clothes. Whenever she helped Ma make candles she was grease from head to toe. She had special old clothes to wear because Ma knew well enough Callie couldn't keep the grease where it belonged.

Right now Mr. Diamond was struggling to get his team of heavy oxen through the doorway of the smithy. One of the bullocks had planted his big splayed front feet against the packed earth of the threshold. He was almost sitting on his hindquarters in furious protest. His staring eyes were bulging. His dripping mouth was open in frantic bellows of fear and anger.

58

Callie could see with half an eye that this was much too interesting to miss.

She put her jug down by a tree and came to stand where she could get a good view of the contest. Carl Oats, the smith, his brawny arms bare, his leather apron shiny with hard use, came up with a heavy chain, which he linked around the wooden yoke resting on the heads of the oxen. He attached the other end to a winch. He and Mr. Diamond threw all of their strength into turning the handle of the big windlass. By inches they got the docile ox and the angry one up onto the forge floor.

"Hey, Callie!" shouted Mr. Diamond. "Throw a bucket of water on the floor in front of them."

Callie lifted the heavy bucket from the bench against the wall and sloshed the water over the floor. The big hoofs slid and slipped on the wet planks. The sullen beasts were windlassed as close as possible to a wooden ox rack of heavy timbers sunk solidly in the floor.

The stubborn ox refused to give up. He fought every inch of the way. Callie felt sorry for him, but she knew he had to be shod.

She watched the two men tie him to the ox-stall and lead the other ox away. Mr. Diamond helped the smith to get a leather apron under the struggling beast. The windlass lifted him, kicking and bellowing, off the floor. His front hoofs were dragged back and chained to heavy rings set in blocks on the floor.

The blacksmith had hammered out the two iron shoes needed for each hoof. Drops of sweat spangled his beard as he caught the jerking right-front hoof and held it between his knees. With infinite patience he nailed the shoe to the scant half inch of slanted hoof.

Mr. Diamond drew Callie outside the forge. "You better run on home, Callie. Tell your ma I'm in town. Tell her to get her tallow ready and a fire going, if she'd like for me to make her some candles. I'll drive up there, soon's I get Pixie shod."

"I'd rather watch," said Callie.

"No," answered Mr. Diamond, rubbing his clean shaven chin. "Carl Oats does a better job when he's free to speak his mind. What Carl has to say to that critter in there is better without a lady in the audience. Carl and Pixie have got three more hoofs to go yet. It's going to be thunderbolts and forked lightning in here before we're done."

Reluctantly Callie picked up her jug. She walked off up the hill with the sounds of Carl Oats' voice raised above the bellows and groans of the outraged ox.

At home she helped Ma build the fire out under the apple trees where the washing was usually boiled. She brought the heavy bags of tallow from the barn and stacked them in the shade. She was glad that Ma had agreed this time to have the candles made. Candlemaking was hot, slow, dangerous and smelly work. It was a chore Callie hated, dipping the candles the way Ma did.

Many years when there were "pinching" times, Ma made all the candles they used, along with the coal-oil lamps. The wicks were dipped over and over again and hung on candle rods to cool and set. But this year there was butter to trade for goods, Pa and the boys were off working for some cash money, and it even looked like a good year for apples.

Callie couldn't believe that one of the patient, slobbering creatures of the ox team that Mr. Diamond drove up to the Dean place later in the morning could be the belligerent and vocal Pixie. The two beasts pulled the painted wagon ponderously around the house to the fire built under the apple trees.

"It's only shoeing makes Pixie mad," said Mr. Diamond. "Somebody must have driven a nail in too close, maybe. Now how about the candles?"

Ma showed Mr. Diamond the carefully saved tallow. He got out his kettles and long-handled dippers. The candle man didn't dip his candles. He poured the tallow into molds. A wick hung down the center of each mold from a nail that rested across the top.

Mr. Diamond took his pay in leftover tallow and food to take along with him—venison and butter, cheese and a glass of Ma's quince preserve.

This time he had come to the Deans' first, so he would go on somewhere else for dinner. But halfway through his work, just before the tallow was ready to pour, Ma sent Callie out to the fire with a plate of dried-apple cake and a mug of sweetened tea.

Mr. Diamond pushed the coals carefully under the kettle of melting grease. He stirred the mess with his long-handled iron dipper. Then he sat down on the washing bench to drink his tea. Callie sat beside him, eating her own slice of cake.

"It's a real pleasure to make candles for your ma," Mr. Diamond told Callie. "She keeps her tallow clean. Some places I get it with meat and hairs and dirt so mixed in, I have to try it all out again, and skim it besides."

"Ma takes a lot of pains with the tallow," agreed Callie. "She tries it out and pours it in the tallow bags before the fat gets rancid. But the candles are still smelly." Callie wrinkled up her nose.

Mr. Diamond nodded. "You can't make a sweet candle out of bear grease and sheep grease, any more than you can make a silk purse out of a ram's tail. I brought some bayberry wax this time. It's made from berries that grow on the East Coast. I'll make a few candles for your ma. They smell sweet and kind of spicy. Tell your ma to save them for a special rincumrumpus, come wintertime."

Mr. Diamond finished his cake and gulped the last of his tea. "Tallow's about ready." He went over to add a piece of wood very carefully to his fire of coals. "Tallow's tricky. You get her too hot, and she'll catch fire. But you got to get her hot enough to pour."

"If you get it too hot when you dip," said Callie, "all the wax you already have on the wick melts off. When you've been dipping for hours, and you've nothing but a greasy wick to show for all your hard work, it's enough to make a body scream."

"Yep," agreed Mr. Diamond. "There's tricks to every trade, and as many to candlemaking as most.

63

Hear you had a holdup in these parts yesterday."

"Yes we did. On the Bootjack Hill."

"Carl Oats said it was some Indian. But Joe Scald, who was the guard on the stage, told me last night he saw the man's wrist when the bandit snatched his gun. Joe says he could see bare skin, and an arm as light as yours or mine, between his glove and the cuff of his sleeve."

Callie jumped up so fast she sent the cake plate spinning. "Mr. Diamond, could Joe Scald swear to that?" she demanded.

"Well now, Callie, I couldn't say as to that. He was pretty excited just talking about it. I'm not sure a judge would take Joe's word for that. You can see all sorts of things when somebody's a-snatching your gun."

This didn't sound very promising, but Callie had felt reasonably sure before now that it couldn't have been Winky who held up the stage. Now she was certain.

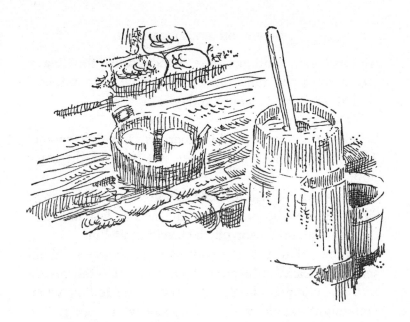

VIII   THE INDIAN CAMP
ON CUSTER CREEK

Callie saw Mr. Diamond and his painted wagon go off down the road. She carried the stacks of newly made candles into the springhouse, where it was cool enough to keep them from melting through the hot months ahead.

Callie's heart sank when she saw her mother getting ready to churn. The morning was gone and Callie still did not have permission to go for berries, where she would be close enough to the Indian camp to warn Tansy.

She'd never get away if she had to help churn. She

watched her mother's sure hands skim the heavy cream from the milk pans into a stoneware pitcher.

"Do we *have* to churn today, Ma?"

"If we want sweet butter we do."

"Could I go for blackberries this afternoon? They're ripe and ready on the hill back of the sawmill."

Ma wouldn't listen. "Not alone," she said firmly. "There's been bears on that hill, late as last fall."

"I can scare a bear off, just yelling at him."

"I don't doubt it, the way you yell. Some of them scare real easy." Ma poured the heavy clotted cream into the wooden churn. "But there's no telling when you might tangle with a she-bear with young. She wouldn't scare worth a cent. She'd tear you to pieces with one swipe."

Callie thought about Tansy and Winky and what the men at the store had been saying. She put her pride in her pocket. "Ma, could I go—if Andy Jensen went?"

Ma fastened down the lid of the churn. She worked the dasher up and down. "Yes," she finally answered. "If you churn this cream until it turns. I'll take it when the butter comes."

Callie plunged the dasher up and down with vim and vigor.

"Easy does it, Callie!" scolded Ma. "You'll have the cream all over the floor. Not too slow and not too fast. Churning has a rhythm. It's like most of the work a woman does, or a man either, for that matter.

Cradle rocking, throwing a shuttle, casting seed. It's done better when it's slow and even."

Callie listened with only half an ear. She was wondering whether Andy would wait for her. She was wondering where to find Tansy if the Indians weren't at Custer Creek. Maybe they'd packed up and gone to the mountains, as many of them did when the hot weather came. Callie hoped they had. Then she wouldn't have to worry about Tansy and Winky. But she had to be sure.

Callie stood at the churn, thumping the dasher up and down. It didn't seem as though the butter would ever come in time for her to meet Andy. Even when the butter and milk had separated and Ma had finished the hard churning, Callie had to stay and pump water while Ma kneaded and worked out the last drops of buttermilk from the yellow mass.

"Cut this in half, Callie." Ma handed her the big loaf of butter. "We'll live rich with the menfolks gone. Press the rest and we'll trade it in."

Callie took the butter into the kitchen to cut it. She wrapped half of it in a clean wet linen square. The rest she pressed into a butter press that had been dipped into cold water. Most of the time Callie liked to press out the round butter pats into a crock of cold water, each round of butter patterned with a golden bee with outspread wings raised upon it.

Today she was impatient to get away. It seemed to take forever to squeeze out the last pat. The crock was emptied of water and lowered into the swift-flowing flume below the kitchen floor, until someone

67

could take the butter pats to town. Ma got good trade value for her sweet, unsalted butter at the store.

The minute the hatch was lowered over the flume, Callie snatched up two pails and a generous heel of bread and fled, before Ma could think of something else for her to do. There was plenty, she knew that. There was all the Saturday cleaning that must be finished by sundown.

She was surprised but pleased to find Andy waiting for her at the bridge, a roll of sausage in one hand and a tin bucket for berries in the other.

"It's about time!" he grumbled. But he exchanged half of his sausage for half of Callie's bread. "We'll have to move fast if we're going to get to Custer Creek and pick berries besides. Can't go home without 'em. Ma had a dozen chores lined up for me."

Callie pushed the handles of her pails up to her elbows. She caught up her skirts in both hands. She was saving her breath. As she started up the hill to the abandoned sawmill, she knew she would have a hard time keeping up with Andy. It wouldn't be easy, she realized almost at once, hampered as she was with two petticoats and four yards of dress skirt.

Back of the sawmill they found a tangled stretch of briars. In the sunny patches, the berries were both ripe-black and glowing red, just right for jelly.

Andy shoved the two pails and the bucket under the bushes. "We'll stop here and pick on the way back. No use hauling pails all the way to the camp."

As they started up the old sawmill road toward Custer Creek, Andy pointed out a circle of second-growth trees. "There's an old stump inside of those trees, ten feet high. From the top of it, straight down, you can see the whole of Hardpan. Through a gap in the hills you can even see the river."

Callie could see the old stump, with a high back to it where the tree had broken off in its fall. "It looks like a throne for a king or a princess."

Andy snorted. "It's just a stump. But you can see the sawmill road for a long ways. On a clear day you can see across the river to the mountains on the other side."

You'd own the whole world from up there, Callie was thinking. She picked up her skirts again to take as long steps as she could to keep up. First chance she got, she decided, she'd come back up here and climb that stump. If you couldn't ride on a stage, she thought, it might be nice to get to where you could see across the river to the hills beyond.

"Come on!" shouted Andy from up ahead. "You're as slow as those globs of molasses!"

Callie stopped thinking about the stump and concentrated all her efforts on getting up the old logging road.

They reached the Indian camp hot and tired. They came over the ridge and could look down on the small meadow on Custer Creek.

The Indian huts, strung along the creek under the sycamores and cottonwoods, were made of brush and poles, covered with frayed cloth sacks or old quilts. There was a smokehouse of wooden slabs, and an open fire or two. Horses were grazing at the head

69

of the clearing. Most of the meadow had been grazed off, but behind a rough fence of unpeeled poles the tall, wild grass stood knee-deep.

There were no Indians in sight.

"They've been here, but they've cleared out," said Andy. "They saw us before we could see them. You go down first, Callie. They all know you. I'll be right behind you."

Callie wasn't afraid, exactly. She knew all of these Indians. Her mother had fed them time and again. Her father had hired many of them to work for him. Half of them wore the Deans' old clothes.

But she felt shy, somehow, in the face of this empty place. There was something creepy about the silent meadow, the abandoned fires. Only the need to warn old Tansy about Winky urged her on.

"Yooo-hooo! Tansy!" she shouted.

The mountain echoed her call. The only sound after this was the bee song, a low thin hum. The meadow remained silent—still. The horses had stopped grazing. They stood like statues, their heads turned to watch Callie and Andy. Not a dog barked. Not a bird chirped. Even their footsteps made no sound in the cropped grass.

Callie stopped and Andy drew up beside her. "What do we do now?" she asked. "Where do you suppose they've gone? How can we find them if they don't want us to?"

"Give her another yell."

Callie put her hands up to her mouth. "Tansy! Tan-zee!"

There was a movement at the end of the meadow. The horses turned to watch as Winky came slowly through the trees, followed by old Tansy.

Callie, with Andy close behind her, walked across the meadow toward the two Indians. "Walk slow," she whispered over her shoulder. "Walk slow. Don't frighten them."

Winky stopped about ten paces away. "What you want?" he demanded. He folded his arms and stood looking at them. In spite of the cheap blanket with a hole cut in it that draped his shoulders, there was a certain dignity about Winky. Old Tansy peered at Callie from behind him.

"Listen, Winky," urged Callie, "we think you'd better get out of here."

"Why you talk Winky?" asked Tansy.

Callie put her hand on the old woman's arm. "Listen, Tansy. Yesterday somebody robbed the stage. You know about the stage, Tansy?"

Tansy nodded.

"Some bad men in town say Winky did it."

The old woman jerked away angrily. Winky did not move or take his eyes from Callie's face.

"No, listen, Tansy," pleaded Callie. "*I* know he didn't do it. Andy does, too, huh?"

"Sure," answered Andy. "We both know you didn't, Winky. But those men—they're stirring up trouble."

"Tansy." Callie's voice was urgent. "You and Winky get away from here until Andy and I can find out who did it. Go up in the mountains. You always go up in summer anyway. Don't wait. Go *now.*"

The old woman stayed still, her bloodshot eyes on Callie, her mouth grim.

Callie put all the pleading she could into her voice. She punched her words into one hand with a clenched fist. "Winky hide. Tom hide. Maybe everybody hide, huh? Until this thing clears up."

"They might throw Winky in jail," added Andy.

Tansy turned on Andy fiercely. "Jail? What Winky do?"

"Nothing, Tansy," answered Callie. "But those men in town are saying he did. They say Winky robbed the stage."

Tansy spat on the ground. "Men lie."

Callie nodded. "I know. But there'll be trouble, Tansy, if you and Winky don't get out of here. Bad trouble."

The old woman stared down at the ground, the wrinkles smoothing out until Callie could see the blue tattoo marks across her face from her dark lips to her ear lobes. Had she understood? It was hard to tell.

When she looked up at Callie again, Tansy's face

73

was a mass of wrinkles once more, her eyes mere slits against the sun.

Callie waited.

Finally Tansy spoke. "Aw right." She turned her back on them and walked off into the trees.

Winky stood where he was, as still as a buck scenting danger.

"Well, I guess it's the best we can do." Callie sighed as she and Andy turned away. "I only hope they understand."

IX MR. PATCH

Callie felt hot and tired and discouraged as she and
Andy started home. How could she be sure that
Tansy understood? What could she and Andy do to
prove that Winky didn't rob the stage? She wished
Pa and the boys were home.

It seemed as though half the town was gone, with
Pa and his three six-foot sons away. Andy wasn't big
enough. It needed Pa and the boys to stand up to
those men in Mr. Hoag's store. They wouldn't pay
any attention to Callie, she felt certain, because she
was a girl.

They stopped under a digger pine to catch their

breath. "How can we prove that Winky didn't rob the stage?" she asked Andy.

"I don't think we can," he answered. "We have to find out who did. They must have the sheriff working on it by now."

"Then what are we supposed to do?" Callie was watching a hawk slowly circling in the blue sky, waiting to come whistling down upon anything that moved.

"Keep Winky out of jail if we can. That's the important thing. Those men at the store don't like the Loosefoots. Jim Turnbeck has taken Cold Spring away from them and he intends to keep it."

"I don't see——" began Callie.

"Then you're stupid," Andy answered shortly. "If they can get that crowd mad enough, they might even hang Winky. That would settle it. If he can just stir the men up enough to get rid of Winky, Jim Turnbeck can keep that land and nobody to hinder."

Callie was furious, but before she could start sputtering Andy had started off. "Come on," he growled. "There's a lot of berries to pick."

He led her down a short cut, a steep and brush-grown trail along a small stream. The long whips of brush slashed at her face. Roots and rocks tripped her feet. Callie caught glimpses of five-fingered ferns dripping over the rocks above the chattering water. Brown bells and the hairy, fawn-colored globes the children called fairy lanterns hung above the woods trash. She must remember this secret garden place. Like the stump this was a place to come back to, she was thinking. Sometime when she didn't have to watch her feet every minute to keep from hurtling down upon Andy. Sometime when Winky was safely away in the hills.

Back of the sawmill, where they picked up their pails, the air was full of the rich, sun-warmed smell of ripe berries, and the bitter smell of yarrow. The berry patch was loud with the hum and buzz of bees.

Callie and Andy were hard at work filling their pails, trying to keep out of reach of the clutching thorns, when Mr. Patch came puffing and blowing up the steep hillside.

"Well met!" he said. "Perhaps you can tell me the way to the Indian camp on Custer Creek."

Callie lowered her heavy pail to the ground. She planted herself in front of him, her hands on her hips. She forgot that this was the schoolmaster. "Why would you want to go to that camp?" she demanded.

Mr. Patch was patting his wet face with his folded handkerchief. "In town they are saying that Winky Loosefoot was the one who robbed the stage."

"He was not!" cried Callie. "Mr. Diamond said the guard could tell it wasn't an Indian."

"Shut up, Callie," said Andy. "I don't think you'll find Winky at the camp, Mr. Patch."

Mr. Patch sighed and went on mopping his forehead and tossing back his lock of unruly hair. "I suppose not. I hope to talk with him before the rest of the men catch up with him. I have brought along every penny I possess to try to buy back my watch. It was my grandfather's watch. I prize it very highly.

I thought if I did not have enough to buy it outright, Winky might let me pay him a little something every quarter. Do you think he might?"

"Winky doesn't have your watch," stated Callie flatly.

"Do you know that for certain, California?"

Callie looked stubborn. "I just know he didn't rob the stage, that's all."

"The men in town feel certain he did," said Mr. Patch. "They are going to get up a *posse comitatus* to hunt him down. They may even kill him. And what good would that do? We'd never find the gold, or the watch either. I thought if I could just talk with him——"

"But, look here, sir," said Andy. "If Winky gave you the watch, it would be the same as saying he was the one who stole the rest of the gold, wouldn't it?"

"I would promise not to divulge the secret. I thought I might be able to convince him that he could never cash in that gold without getting caught. I hoped to persuade him to take it to the sheriff at Bootjack."

"He doesn't have it," said Callie. "Anyway, there isn't anybody at the camp. We only saw Tansy because I'm a friend of hers."

"Have you been up there to see them?" asked Mr. Patch.

There was a frightened silence. Neither Callie nor Andy answered.

"I suppose," said Mr. Patch, "you went up there to warn them?"

Still neither of them spoke.

"I might have done the same," said Mr. Patch, "if I felt as you do. I meant to tell them myself that they had better get away. Only I hoped to get my watch back first."

"Winky hasn't got it. He didn't do it." Callie's voice was cross. "Come on, Andy, we'd better pick berries."

Mr. Patch sat down on a stump, fanning his flushed face with his hat. He didn't seem to know what to do, where to turn.

"Weren't there any men on the stage to guard the gold?" asked Andy as he went on with his berry picking.

"Yes," answered Mr. Patch. "There was an armed guard beside the driver. But the stage had an extra heavy load. All of us beside the driver and the guard got out to lighten the load up that steep hill. An armed man, hidden beneath a sack, held the stage up while it waited for us to climb the hill. The guard was half asleep. The bandit had the gold and his gun before we got there. He had a bead on us as we came around the road. He took all our money and valuables. I didn't have much money, but he made me put my watch in the sack he had put on the ground."

"Didn't he say anything so you could tell if it was Winky?"

"No. He didn't talk. He just motioned with his gun. That is a very potent argument, Andy. And he wore gloves."

79

"Gloves!" snorted Callie. "That's another thing. Where in the world would Winky get gloves? How can you possibly think it was Winky?"

"Because he was wearing moccasins," said Mr. Patch sadly. "Moccasins with pink porcupine quills embroidered on them, like the ones that Tansy makes."

Moccasins! Callie's heart sank. Everybody on the stage must have seen them. Against the word of one startled, sleep-dazed guard who had seen a wrist between sleeve and glove while a man was snatching his gun, there was the damning evidence of a pair of moccasins embroidered with pink porcupine quills.

Callie had her second pail half full when they heard hoofbeats coming up the road from Hardpan. Callie could see the men through the trees, nine or ten of them, riding two-by-two. They had guns in their hands, and beneath their hat brims their bearded faces were grim. They did not even glance up at the berry patch as they spurred their horses up the road toward the Indian camp on Custer Creek.

Mr. Patch was staring after them. "I'm afraid it is too late to hope to get my watch back now," he was saying unhappily. "They'll kill Winky, and I'll never know what became of it."

"They won't ever catch him," declared Callie. "Tansy won't let them. You wait and see."

But before they were down the mountain, they heard the horses behind them. Andy and Callie and Mr. Patch crowded over on the narrow road to let the riders by. They could see Winky in the middle

of them, his hands tied behind him, his long black hair hanging in lank wisps over his bent head. He no longer had dignity. He looked dejected, discouraged, beaten.

Callie pounded her clenched hands against a tree. "He didn't do it!" she stormed. "I just know he didn't."

Mr. Patch patted her shoulder. "What makes you so sure, California?"

Callie brushed her arm fiercely across her flushed face. "Because Tansy wouldn't let him. The Indians haven't had a chance since Mr. Hoag and Jim Turnbeck came in here. Tansy hauls that big baby around so Winky's wife can wash clothes all day. Sometimes she gets paid and half the time she doesn't. Nobody hires Winky and Tom any more, because Mr. Hoag says they're not honest. Pa used to, and he would now, but my brothers are big enough to help."

Callie stopped for breath.

"And you think Winky wouldn't be tempted by all that gold on the stage?" asked Mr. Patch.

"Of course not! What could he *do* with it? Any Indian turning up with smelted gold would be clapped into jail."

"I'm inclined to think you are right," said Mr. Patch.

Callie stared at him.

"Loyalty is a rare thing," said Mr. Patch. "Anyone who can inspire such unswerving loyalty could not possibly rob a stage. I am convinced of it."

But the men in Mr. Hoag's store were not convinced. They had found Winky at Custer Creek, where the Indians were packing their pitiful belongings on their horses.

In spite of Callie's and Andy's long trip to the camp on Custer Creek to warn the Indians, the men had brought Winky back to Hardpan and locked him in the jail.

X THE SWING ACROSS
SAWMILL CREEK

The Sunday morning, after Winky had been locked
up, the whole town was seething. Most of the old-
timers agreed with Callie's mother. "It's ridiculous!"
said Ma. "Winky has better sense than to steal gold
he couldn't spend."

Mrs. Jensen said, "It iss not enough to hang a
man on de say-so of dese loafers."

The men who had captured Winky were all for
stringing him up to the nearest tree. But the old-
timers and a few men like Mr. Patch and Mr. Jensen
demanded a fair trial.

They sent to Bootjack for the sheriff. They fitted up the second room of the Hardpan jail with a cot where the sheriff could sleep. They put a comfortable chair outside, so he could sit tilted back against the stone wall and whittle in the shade. He had a gun on either hip and a glint in his eye. The sheriff had every intention of keeping Winky in, and the men who wanted to hang him, out.

The town was split into two camps. Most of the men who hung about the saloon and Mr. Hoag's store wanted Winky hanged and no nonsense.

Most of the women in town, including Ma and Mrs. Jensen, didn't believe for one minute that Winky had stolen the gold. They were against impromptu hangings as well. Backing them was a tight little group of men who, whether they believed Winky guilty or not, held that justice in California demanded an honest trial.

"We have outgrown these hangings," said Mr. Jensen.

"The days of Judge Lynch must be replaced by sanity and fair judgment," thundered Mr. Patch from his desk, which was the pulpit on Sunday.

Callie felt better with Winky in jail, and the sheriff on guard, than she had since she first heard of the holdup. But if she thought for a moment that her quarrel with Andy Jensen had been patched up because of their mutual concern for Winky, Andy soon put her straight.

Monday morning Callie was under the apple trees, spreading the first tubful of wash on the bushes, when she saw Andy and Willie Binks going by along the flume. Andy had a coil of heavy rope over one arm.

"Yoo-hoo!" yelled Callie. "Where you going with that rope?"

Willie Binks waved and shouted something, but Andy stalked on without turning his head.

"He says it's none of your business," shouted Willie gleefully.

Callie went about the rest of her morning's work like a whirlwind. What were the boys doing with that rope? She wiped dishes with a lick and no promise. Where were Andy and Willie headed? She swept the broad planks of the kitchen floor so fast and so hard that her mother stopped her in the middle.

"If you're going to put that much into it," she told Callie, "wet the broom first!"

It was nearly noon when Sue Ellen Binks appeared at the front door.

"Can Callie come play with me? I got nobody kin play."

"Where'd the boys go?" asked Callie.

"They have it in mind to hist a rope over that big oak up the crik. To swing theirselves across."

Callie looked at Ma with pleading eyes.

"Oh, all right!" Ma gave her a little push. "You've stirred things up here until it will take the rest of the day to mop and dust. If you land in the creek, you'll have to wash and iron your own clothes. And don't forget, Callie, I need you later this afternoon to help me spread berries. Tansy brought me baskets of berries. I've jelled all I have jars for. I'll dry the rest."

Callie sighed. Summertimes boys could go off with ropes or fishing tackle, or into the forests to fell trees. Vacation for a girl was just a lot more work.

She and Sue Ellen set off up the Sawmill Creek road, chewing busily on thick slices of bread spread with sweet butter and mashed blackberries thickened with sugar.

It was a perfect day, with a sky so blue it made Callie's heart ache for anyone, like Winky, shut up in a stone jail. Below the road Sawmill Creek, swollen with melted snow, surged over the rocks and roots, shadowed by leaning trees, dragging long sprays of briars in green loops along the edges.

They could hear the shouts up ahead long before they got to the big oak. They could see the long rope tied to a high limb over the creek. They saw Andy catch the swinging rope one of the boys had sent over to where he stood on the opposite bank. With a run and jump he hurled himself across to the other side in a long arc.

Below the steep banks of the stream, the water was deep and swift. Several of the smaller boys were wet and muddy. Willie Binks had torn the knee patch off his pants and had skinned his knee as well. They all seemed happy and unconcerned, laughing and shouting, as they waited their turn.

Andy swung swiftly back across the creek, as Sue

87

Ellen and Callie came up, landing neatly on his feet in front of them.

"Who said you could come up here?" he demanded.

"Well, and who said we couldn't?" Callie didn't mean to start out like this, but Andy always got her riled.

"We don't want any girls around," shouted Willie from across the creek. "Girls are sissy."

"You don't own this here land, Smarty," his sister pointed out. "It's just as much ourn, if we feel like it."

"Maybe the land is," taunted Andy, "but the rope isn't." He caught the swinging rope. He turned his back on Callie, wrapped his big hands above the knot at the end, gave a little run and jump, and went swinging across to the other side.

Callie stuffed the last of her bread and blackberries in her mouth and sat down below the oak tree. Let Andy be mean, she thought. This was better than sweeping and dusting.

The sun filtered down through the oak leaves and danced on the swift-flowing water of Sawmill Creek. The bank behind her was starred with flowers and dripping with ferns under a fallen giant of a dead tree with a tremendous spread of roots. The ground underfoot was spongy with last year's leaves and pine needles.

It must be simply wonderful to see how far you could swing on that long rope, Callie thought.

The urge to try that glorious swing grew greater

by the minute. She could see that the boys had no intention of giving up the rope. Each boy turned it over to the next one. As the last boy on one side finished his swing over and back, he sent the knotted rope across to the other bank. Andy kept a wary eye on Callie when it was on her side of the stream.

The boys shouted and showed off and all but turned inside out in their efforts to attract attention and to prove that this was the most fun they'd ever had.

Callie sat back against the mossy bank in a tangle of oak roots. She closed her eyes until she could just peek through her long eyelashes. They couldn't tell where Callie was looking. She knew it would spoil half their fun if she didn't watch. Let them guess what she was thinking. They knew well enough she was trying to figure out how to get that rope.

She couldn't do it by force. She had tangled often enough with Andy to know that his long arms could always hold the rope just out of her reach. She had to admit that he was stronger than she was and wouldn't hesitate to shove her out of his way.

She couldn't see how she could outwit him either. Andy, as the biggest boy, had stayed on her side of the creek. She couldn't think of any ruse that would get her close enough to snatch the rope.

She could wait until the boys tired of the swinging, and went home. But what fun would that be? This was the kind of game that needed an audience.

Besides, Andy was ornery enough to take the rope home with him.

The only thing left was to buy a ride. The minute she thought of it, she remembered the obsidian skinning knife. Any boy in town would like to own that shining black knife. Was it worth it? Hadn't she just about outgrown arrowheads and skinning knives? Wasn't she going to turn them all over to Sma' John one of these days?

Callie looked around the bank in back of her. High on the bank there was the giant fallen tree with its spreading roots crusted with dirt. She measured the distance across the creek from the tree to a high, flat rock bedded in the steep hillside behind the opposite bank. Could she make it across to that rock if she jumped from the dead tree? She wasn't absolutely sure, but it was worth a try.

She wished she had brought the skinning knife with her. She was sure that just showing it would do the trick. But she didn't want to go home and get it. Ma would put her to work straight off, spreading berries.

Andy wouldn't want anyone else to have it. Next to Callie he had the best arrowhead collection in town. She'd have to do some tall talking without the knife. She could see that.

Callie sat with half-closed eyes, while the boys shouted and showed off. She was spinning plans. She meant to keep her knife and ride on the swing besides.

XI THE HIGH PRICE
OF A LONG SWING

The next time Andy finished his turn Callie sat up
and opened her eyes. "Do you think Winky's safe
in that jail, Andy?" she asked innocently.

Andy gave her a quick glance. "Safe enough."

"Ma says she thinks they'll have a hard time finding a judge to try him."

Andy didn't answer.

Callie tried again. "Joe Scald, the guard on that
stage, told Mr. Diamond he saw the wrist of the
holdup man, and it wasn't an Indian."

"Tell it to the sheriff," said Andy, his voice bored.

"Maybe I will," she answered. "That's a very good suggestion."

"It's your turn, Willie," shouted Andy. "Here she comes."

"You know that black skinning knife Winky gave me?" asked Callie.

The question caught Andy unawares. Callie could see that he was looking at this new approach from all sides. She fastened her gaze on the high rock across the creek, resisting the fierce urge to look back at the fallen tree.

"What about it?" asked Andy cautiously.

"Nothing. Only I thought I might give it to Sma' John for his birthday."

Andy's voice was full of anguish. "Sma' John's too little. He'd just lose it. Are you crazy?"

Callie shrugged. "Well, I don't want it so much any more." She stood up, smothered a yawn, and smoothed down her dress. "Come on, Sue Ellen, let's go home. There's nothing to do here."

"Ain't we ever goin' to git a ride?" asked Sue Ellen. "That's what we come for."

Callie spread her hands out and stuck out her lower lip. "The boys won't let us. Come on home. I'll show you my arrowhead collection. Winky gave me a good drill last week."

Andy moved closer. "That skinning knife——" he began.

Callie turned away from him to watch the boy backing up for his running start on the long swing across the creek.

94

"Callie——" said Andy.

"Don't let me interfere with your rope swing, Andy, if it's your turn. It looks like a lot of fun. Come on, Sue Ellen. I have a jim-dandy arrowhead I'll give you—now I'm giving things away."

"You really goin' to give that skinning knife away?" Andy wanted to know.

"I might—why?" Callie kept her voice casual. "You know——" She looked across to the high flat rock bedded on the bank above where the boys were clustered around the rope. "I bet I could swing across to the top of that rock on that rope," she said in a rush.

Andy looked at the rock and snorted. "Aw! You could not!"

"Well, I bet I can. I bet you—let me see—I'll bet you my skinning knife that I can make it."

She let the long pause lengthen. She could see that Andy knew that he couldn't make it from where he stood. So of course she couldn't. "I just bet you could not," he said scornfully.

"I'll bet you my skinning knife."

Andy wavered. "What do you want for it?" But he knew well enough.

"A ride on the rope whenever I like," coaxed Callie.

Andy hated to give in—but that skinning knife! "Whenever it's your turn," he agreed grudgingly.

Callie's face was still, except for the dimple flickering in her chin. She'd show that Andy.

"Me, too?" demanded Sue Ellen. "Me, too?"

95

"Sue Ellen, too," said Callie firmly.

Andy winced. "All right," he grunted. He raised his voice. "The girls can swing, too."

A chorus of boos and catcalls answered him, but Andy silenced them. "It's my rope," he shouted.

Callie waited for her turn with patience. She watched each boy to see how he held the rope above the knot, how he gave a run and shove before he lifted his feet for the long swing. There would be no run from that dead tree. She'd have to jump as high as she could to make up for it.

The next time Andy came back swiftly on the return trip and handed the rope over to her with a mocking bow. "It's yours, ma'am." He couldn't resist adding, "And the skinning knife is mine."

"Don't be too sure," answered Callie. She grabbed the rope, caught up her long skirts, and began to climb the clogged roots of the dead tree.

"Hey, Callie!" yelled Andy. "You crazy? You'll break your fool neck. Come down off of there."

Callie scrambled on, pushing her way up between the great spreading roots. She lifted her dress off one snag. She knocked her knee and tore her stocking on another. She snatched her shoe out of Andy's clutch and sent a shower of dirt down into his upturned face.

When she reached the trunk of the high tree, her heart froze. It was terrifying to look down, dismaying to look across. All of them, Andy, Sue Ellen, the boys were as still as though they were playing a game of "Still-pond-no-more-moving."

The rushing water below her looked deep and cold. The high rock across the creek stood granite hard and far.

A blue jay in a tree above her gave a frantic squawk and sailed across the creek into the trees. Callie wished she had wings and a squawk to match.

"Callie! Callie Dean! You come down off of there!" Andy's voice was furious and scared at the same time.

That did it. Callie wrapped her hands around the rope as far above the big knot as she could reach and jumped. She swung her legs up and sailed out over the creek, her hands slipping on the heavy rope.

The rock came rushing at her.

"Swing up!" shouted Andy. "Twist! Twist and swing!"

Callie twisted in the air, swung her whole body up, and cleared the rock by a scant inch.

"Let go!" shouted Andy.

Callie let go. She rolled onto the pine needles and twigs on top of the rock with the breath all but knocked out of her. She lay there, sucking air into her lungs and feeling all over to see if there were any broken bones.

She was jarred and breathless, but as soon as she was sure she was all in one piece she clambered to her feet. She saw the rope come swinging back as she began to climb down the hillside in back of the rock.

Below her she could see a blur of faces staring

up at the rock where she had landed. She slid the rest of the way down the bank in a shower of damp earth.

The rope was swinging idly back and forth over the middle of the stream.

Andy looked disgusted. "Come on, everybody," he shouted. "Let's go up and take a swim."

As one man the boys turned away from Callie and the rope. They set off up Sawmill Creek, headed, Callie knew, for the old mill dam. This was a place where girls couldn't follow.

Callie walked slowly down stream. Sue Ellen did the same on the opposite bank. Callie's head was spinning. Her back felt wrenched. One knee was stiff and bruised. Her stocking was torn and her clothes were caked with dirt. She dreaded facing Ma.

It was true, she had shown Andy she could swing across to the big rock—something he hadn't even thought of doing himself. She had won back her skinning knife as she had planned to do. But she had lost her audience. Her moment of golden triumph had turned to brass in her mouth.

Callie joined Sue Ellen at the upper bridge. "I'm real sorry you didn't get a turn, Sue Ellen."

"It makes no never mind," answered Sue Ellen stoutly. "I'd have landed most like in the crik, and I'd sure catch it for that."

Callie felt cross and rebellious. It wasn't fair. A boy could go home dirty and wet, and nobody cared. He could go off on a hot summer day to swing on a rope or swim in the mill pond, and nobody said a word. A girl had to wash and iron her muddied clothes, and if she landed in the creek she'd catch it when she got home.

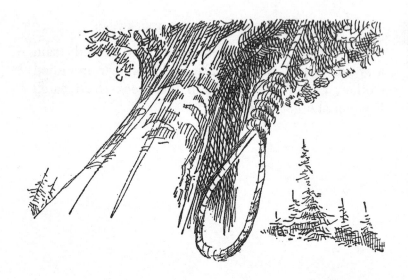

XII "A NICE LONG HANGIN' ROPE"

Callie and Sue Ellen wandered along under the
locust trees. Neither of them wanted to go home to
face certain employment for the rest of the afternoon.

They could see a lot of men gathered outside of
Mr. Hoag's store, sitting on the steps, leaning against
the porch rail and the hitching rail. They were
arguing, boasting, shouting with laughter one minute, muttering and cursing the next.

One man pointed toward the sawmill trail. The
muttering changed to growls as Tansy Loosefoot
came down the road.

Tansy plodded by the men at the store, looking neither to right nor to left. In her hands she carried an Indian basket.

"What you got there—you?" one of the men shouted.

Tansy stared him down.

"Acorn mush for Winky, I think," Callie whispered to Sue Ellen.

The sheriff ran his finger down into the basket. "Got to see if you're bringing in anything illegal, Tansy. Looks pretty good. Next time bring me some."

Tansy showed her toothless gums in a wintry smile. She handed the sheriff the basket and sat down outside the jail.

There was the sound of hoofbeats on the road. Jim Turnbeck came riding in on a jaded sorrel, leading a loaded pack train of mules. The packer stopped his horse in front of the store. "Whoa, there!" he drawled as the laden mules pulled up, pushing and shoving, crowding against each other.

Nearly everyone, except Callie, liked Jim Turnbeck. She didn't like him because he had run the Indians off their land, but she had to admit he had a jolly laugh. One eye was half closed but the other twinkled merrily. His drooping mustache and drooping eye and the sideburns halfway down his cheek somehow gave him a comical air.

Nobody liked Mr. Hoag, Callie was thinking, because he seemed sly and sneaky and forevermore sticky. But Jim Turnbeck got people laughing with his quips and dancing with his fiddle.

There was a dried rattlesnake skin around his broad-brimmed hat and a bright red kerchief above a flowered vest. His skin was burned brick red by wind and sun, and every time Callie had seen him his eyelashes were white with trail dust. His hair was long and black and luxuriant and he kept it well oiled with bear's grease. When he took his hat off, an oily, muddy band marked his forehead where the sweat band of his hat had rested.

Jim Turnbeck played his fiddle and spoke up real lively when he called the dances for the wingdings on the hard-packed earth of the parade ground. The rest of the time his voice was lazy. He slouched lazy in the saddle. He walked lazy and bowlegged on the ground.

Right now he sat in his saddle and looked over the group of men with lazy amusement. "Wall, what are you waitin' for? There's a rope hanging thirty feet down from that big oak up the trail. Looks like it's just askin' for a neck to stretch."

"What rope?"

"Who put it there?"

"How should I know? I been gone for a week." He got off his horse and tied it to the hitching rail. He slapped the dusty rump of a black mule. "Git over—you! All I know is somebody did. Who else would anybody have in mind, with a nice long hangin' rope, but a thieving Indian?"

Callie stopped in her tracks. "Sue Ellen!" she whispered. "That's all they need. A rope hanging to a tree."

"What you aim to do, Callie?"

"I'm going back to pull down that rope. You go on home, Sue Ellen." There was no use telling Sue Ellen not to tell anyone what she had in mind, but Sue Ellen was better off at home.

"Oo-oo! Callie! That rope's a ways up in that tree. It's terrible far up. How about gettin' Andy?"

"No time. Some of these men will go up there to get that rope. Then they'll hang Winky for sure."

"But, Callie—suppose they see you gittin' that rope?"

Callie snorted. She gave Sue Ellen a push toward home and turned back through town. She walked as fast as she dared until she had passed the blacksmith shop. She began to run as soon as she was sure she was out of sight of the men in town.

She reached her own gate, winded. She could see her mother and Sma' John out behind the kitchen. Her mother was setting up sawhorses with planks for the berry drying.

Callie unbuttoned her shoes. She left them on the bridge at the foot of the garden. She flew up the path in her stocking feet, keeping well out of sight of the kitchen and back yard. She rummaged through a drawer, up in her own room, until she found the skinning knife. She put it in the deep pocket of her dress.

Callie hoped to untie the rope. She didn't want to cut it if she could help it. Rope cost money, and it wasn't her rope. But she was afraid the knot would be too tight to untie after all the swinging.

At the bridge she pulled on her shoes, stopping only to button the top buttons. She ducked down below the willows and tall grasses along the flume to keep out of sight.

She was hoping she might find the boys back at the oak, now that she and Sue Ellen were gone. But the rope hung limp from the high limb above the water. It swayed a little in a wind that rustled the grasses on the hillside above and turned the cottonwood leaves to silver against the green. There was no one there. No one at all.

The oak looked high and forbidding. Callie set her jaw. "If Andy Jensen can climb it, I can climb it," she muttered. Only thing was, she was thinking, Andy wasn't hampered by yards and yards of dress and petticoats.

The boys had cut a small sapling and braced it against the oak tree. Callie shucked off her shoes and shinnied up the leaning tree. From there to where the rope was tied was harder going. There were some stretches that must have taxed even Andy's long reach. Crawling out on the limb over the creek was the worst of all. The rushing water far below made her feel lightheaded and dizzy.

She was glad she had brought the skinning knife. She could see, without even feeling it, that the knot was too tight to untie. It wasn't going to be easy to cut either. She needed one hand to hold on, even with her feet hooked around the limb.

The edge of the broad knife of black glass had felt as sharp as a steel blade when Winky had given it to her. Now it seemed a dull tool that would take forever to saw through each strand of the heavy rope.

Callie didn't want to be caught taking the rope down. She didn't want the men who had been talking to Jim Turnbeck to find either the rope or Callie Dean up in the oak tree. She was afraid that if she let it fall into the water below, it would be carried down stream in plain sight of anyone coming up the trail. She wasn't sure whether rope like this was light enough to float until it became waterlogged. She hated to think of that tempting rope floating through Hardpan, to be gathered in by the first man who spied it.

Andy wasn't going to be pleased to see his rope cut as it was. He would be furious to lose it.

Callie took time out to haul the rope up into the tree and drape it around over other limbs, so it wouldn't fall when she cut through it. Then she settled down grimly to the slow grinding business of cutting the rope, strand by strand, with the rough edge of the skinning knife.

She expected every minute to hear voices from down the trail. What was keeping the men? The sheriff maybe, she thought. Perhaps the men were trying to get Winky out of jail to bring him up here with them. Well, down there they'd have Tansy to reckon with. And they wouldn't find a rope hanging handy, if Callie Dean could help it.

The last strand of the rope parted so suddenly the surprise almost threw Callie out of the tree.

She managed to get the skinning knife back in her pocket. She had cut the rope, but now there was an awful lot of it dangling around the nearby limbs of the oak. Callie knew it was perfectly visible from down below.

This time she did hear voices, but not from the direction of Hardpan. There was a howl of wrath from the upper trail.

"Hey, look, Andy! Somebody went and took down our rope!"

"I bet it was Callie!" Andy's voice was hoarse with outrage.

"You can see it up there."

"It's all tangled up."

"It's still up the tree, Andy."

"So's Callie. You just wait, Callie Dean!"

Callie sat straddled on the limb, like riding a bucking horse. "Stop your noise!" she shouted. "I'll drop the rope down, and you get it away from here. Those men in town are coming up here any minute to hang Winky with it."

"You sure?"

"Sure. Jim Turnbeck saw it and he told them it was here." Callie was pulling down the loops of rope, working it over to the side of the tree away from the stream.

"Drop it down then," ordered Andy. "And get down here yourself."

That bossy Andy! What did he think she was doing? Callie unwrapped the last loop of rope and let it drop.

"Here, Willie," said Andy, "you and the rest of you get this rope out of sight. Hide it in the bushes up the creek. Come on down, Callie."

Callie sat on the high limb and watched the boys hastily loop up the rope and go running up the trail with it.

"Callie!" yelled Andy. "Come on down. You want to get caught up there?"

Callie sat right where she was. It didn't matter so much being caught up in the tree, now that the rope was gone. She was pretty sure none of the men hanging around Hoag's store could climb a tree. The truth of it was, she didn't intend to climb down in front of Andy.

There were shouts from the direction of Hardpan.

Andy started down that way. "I'll go down trail and hold them off, Callie, while you climb down out of there."

Callie scrambled down from the oak tree. She put on her shoes and hurried down the trail to where Andy was talking to three men. "There isn't any rope hanging up anywhere around here, I tell you," Andy was saying.

"Jim Turnbeck said there was."

"He was joking, maybe." Andy caught sight of Callie. He stopped arguing. "All right. Go up and see for yourselves," he told them.

He stalked off down the trail. Callie followed him. Just like an old squaw, thought Callie with a gurgle of laughter. She felt lightheaded and foolishly gay now that the rope was gone.

Callie hoped Andy would tell her he thought she had been smart to get the rope down by herself in time. But he didn't. They walked along in glum silence. Callie could see that Andy hadn't forgiven her for the swing across the creek to the high rock. She tossed her head. Let him sulk, for all she cared. He hadn't even thought of that old dead tree for a take-off, or the high rock for a landing. And it wasn't Andy who got the rope down.

A sudden doubt struck Callie. Maybe that was part of the trouble between her and Andy. Maybe boys didn't like to have girls beat them at their own games. Maybe Andy resented Callie because she could do most things as well as he could and some of them, like slinging mud balls, even better.

Well, let him be mad. She'd show that Andy!

Callie left him at her own gate and went around in back of the house.

"I must say it's about time!" said her mother. Ma brushed the strands of hair from her face with fingers stained purple with fruit juice.

Callie waved away a bee and began shaking berries from a pail onto the sunlit planks.

"Sue Ellen was here half an hour ago to see if you were home." Ma's voice was exasperated. "She said something about the men and Winky. Where ever have you been?"

"Up the trail a ways."

"What were you doing all that time?"

"Nothing much." Callie sucked the dark juice of a squashed berry from her fingers. She looked up at the brown hill above the upper pasture. The stacked hay looked almost silver in the afternoon light, she was thinking. She brought her thoughts back to her mother's question. "Swinging on a rope, mostly."

"I declare!" said Ma. "Seems to me, Callie, you get more scatterbrained by the day."

"Yes, ma'am," answered Callie.

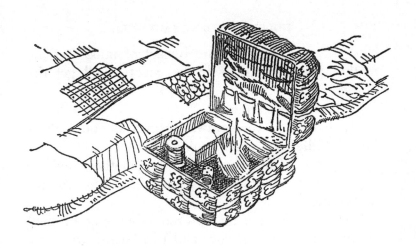

XIII CALLIE TRIES
TO THINK

The next afternoon Ma put her silver thimble and precious steel needle in her black sewing case embroidered with blue forget-me-nots. She tied a bonnet under her chin and a Paisley shawl around Sma' John.

"I am going over to the Jensens' to help quilt, Callie," said Ma. "I'm taking Sma' John with me. I'll put him down for his nap over there. Keep an eye on the stove. Don't let the beans stop boiling or they'll be tough. Bring the cow into the barn if I am not back by four. But don't you try to milk. I can't afford to lose another bucket of milk. Get the mother hen cooped up or the coyotes will get the chicks."

Callie nodded absently.

Ma looked at the faraway expression on Callie's face. "Callie! Are you listening?"

"Yes, Ma." Callie had heard her mother, but she was turning over and over in her mind the problem of Winky.

The jail was a solid two-room building of field stone. It had an iron door and two barred windows. Winky was in one room and his door was kept locked. The sheriff was sleeping in the outer room, and sitting outside in the shade during the daytime. He went over to the eating house to get his meals, but he locked the outer jail door before he left.

No, Callie was thinking as she shoved a heavy chunk of oak wood in the stove, there was no way she and Andy could get Winky out of the jail. The only thing they could do was to find out who had robbed the stage.

But how could they? The bandit had been well covered, a sack over his head with just slits for eyeholes. He had herded all of the passengers into the stage after robbing them of money and valuables. He had fired his gun close to the head of the lead horse. As the team bolted, the passengers had seen the masked man drag the box into the trees by the side of the road.

Mr. Diamond said the guard was pretty sure the bandit was not an Indian. But he wasn't sure enough to swear to it. You had to be dead sure, Callie was thinking, with men like the hangers-on at Mr. Hoag's store. They wanted it to be Winky.

The stage robber was probably far away by now, in some hide-out in the mountains, just waiting for someone to hang Winky before he began spending all that gold. Thinking of distant hide-outs, Callie thought of the stump above the sawmill. From the top of that stump, you could see all of Hardpan and across the Sacramento Valley to the mountains on the other side. Maybe if she could see those distant hills beyond, she could think of something to help Winky. The stump seemed to be a good place to think.

Callie forgot the beans and the cow and the mother hen. She cut herself a huge slice of bread, lathered it with sweet unsalted butter, and sprinkled it with a thick layer of coarse brown sugar. Chewing thoughtfully, she set off up the hill on the sawmill trail.

The stump wasn't easy to climb. But anyone who could climb a sixty-foot oak could manage to surmount a ten-foot stump, even with slabs of bark peeling off when she was clinging to them. The stump was an exciting place. Callie could see the thin silver thread of the river through a gap in the hills. She could see another range of mountains in the far distance, blue and remote against the sky.

It was a wonderful high place to be, half hidden by the circle of trees and ringed around by sun-warmed canyon slopes. The town of Hardpan looked small and far away and not like itself, seen from above. The schoolhouse looked as small as a doll's house. Even the blacksmith's shop, at this end of the main street, seemed to have shrunk.

Callie sat cross-legged on the stump and tried to think. Mr. Patch had said she hadn't learned to think. She was afraid he was right. No matter how she turned the problem of Winky over in her mind, she couldn't find an answer.

A high dead tree, across the road, its bark long since stripped, stood out in a silver-white twist against the sky. An eagle or a large hawk sat hunched and still on the top of it. As Callie watched, he spread noiseless wings and swooped off across the timbered canyon, riding the wind. Callie thought of Winky, another wild-bred creature, walled up in a stone jail.

There were faint rustlings in the underbrush behind the stump. A quail called, "Not quite yet!" and again, "Not quite yet!" Callie saw the mother quail wait a bit before she shooed the babies, not much bigger than Ma's silver thimble, across the road and into the brush.

At the same moment she heard voices and caught a movement on the sawmill road close at hand. She peered between the trees until she could see that the two men coming down the road were Mr. Hoag and Jim Turnbeck. Callie could hear their voices as they passed close below her. She shrank back against the high back of the stump, but neither of them looked up at the circle of trees.

Mr. Hoag was talking in his whining voice. "—and I'm in favor of draggin' Winky out of there, if the sheriff don't set trial by Thursday."

"But Thursday's only day after tomorrow," drawled Jim Turnbeck. "I say let things take their course. The men'll get mad enough by themselves. They'll have him out of there when they get good and ready. They're itchin' for trouble."

"I'm not in favor of all this foolin' around," answered Mr. Hoag stubbornly. "I'll wait until Thursday, an' that's all."

The rest of his words were lost to Callie as a small wind set the trees above her to murmuring softly.

Callie hadn't been too much worried as long as Winky had seemed safe in the jail. But now he wouldn't be safe. Not after Thursday. If the sheriff hadn't set trial by day after tomorrow, Mr. Hoag would see that the men at the store took matters into their own hands.

Again Callie wished with all her heart that Pa and the boys were home. Pa wouldn't sit around and let anyone harm Winky. Pa and his three boys were solid. Pa had a way of settling things quiet and peaceable. People like Mr. Hoag and Jim Turnbeck had to listen to John Dean, backed up by his three six-foot sons.

Callie sighed. She missed her brothers. Somehow, in the last year or so, they had turned into grown men. Matt and Mark at sixteen and Luke at fifteen had left Callie far behind, only eleven. It seemed to

Callie that she had been eleven for years and years and years.

Through the late afternoon quiet she heard the heavy clank of a cowbell. She remembered the cow! And the beans! And the mother hen fending off a whole clutch of coyotes!

She slid down off the stump so fast she tore a hole in her ribbed stockings and skinned her banged-up knee. She was muttering as she plunged headlong down the road, "The reason you never get to be more than eleven, Callie Dean, is because you don't have *sense* enough to grow up."

To her surprise, thanks to the heavy oak chunk she had put in the stove, the beans were still bubbling. The mother hen was guarding her baby chicks against everything, including Callie.

She finally managed to get the cranky old biddy safe under the coop and the chicks safe under her wings.

Mr. Patch was waiting for her at the gate of the hill meadow when she came back with the cow. "Have you heard what the men are saying?" he asked as he held the gate open for her.

"Yes," she said unhappily. "I heard Mr. Hoag say they'll wait until Thursday, and that's all. Can't the sheriff stop them?"

"Not if they really mean it. He couldn't hold out, one man against a whole mob, could he?"

"I guess not. But what can we do?"

"Tell me, California, is it true that you saw Winky

and Tom together that afternoon, and that Winky went over the hill on the Bootjack trail?"

Callie pressed her lips together. Nobody was going to get *that* out of her.

Mr. Patch chuckled. "So you did."

"I didn't say that! You can't——"

"There was no need to. Your face is an open book. I am on your side, California, remember? It might be better for us to try to work together."

Callie faced him. "All right. It's true. But you have to promise not to tell. Please don't tell. If the sheriff has anybody's word but Mr. Hoag's to prove that Winky went over that hill Friday afternoon, it—well—it would just be the end of Winky."

"Yes, it easily might," Mr. Patch agreed. "Tell me this. Would there have been time, after you saw him, for Winky to get far enough along the trail to see the stage on the Bootjack Hill?"

Callie nodded miserably. "Andy caught the stage last year, even after it had left Hardpan. And Friday afternoon Winky started off up that trail before the stage even got here."

"Do you think Winky might have seen the holdup? Let us say he was on that hill above the Bootjack road. That's cut-over land. Wouldn't anyone on the trail be able to see most of that road?"

Suddenly Callie began to see what Mr. Patch had in mind. Of course Winky must have seen the holdup.

"But could he have seen the bandit if the man had a sack over his head?"

"It is difficult to say. He might have seen the

man before he put on the sack. You know how curious the Indians are, and how quietly they can watch."

Callie tied up the cow. Her head was in a whirl. "Winky might even have followed the man after the holdup."

"A distinct possibility. You see, California? Two heads are better than one. Now—Winky wouldn't listen to me, would he, if I were to question him? Or to Andy?"

"He might listen to you, Mr. Patch, or to Andy, either one. But I don't really think he would tell you anything."

"Would he tell you?"

Callie thought about this for a frowning moment. "I don't rightly know. I've never talked to Winky much. I'm afraid he'd think it was a trap."

"Could you talk to Tansy? Could you get her to question Winky?"

"I can always talk to Tansy. I'm never sure how much she understands."

Callie and Mr. Patch walked out to the front gate, both of them studying the problem. Callie was thankful to have someone else to help her think.

"California," said Mr. Patch when they reached the gate, "see if you can persuade Tansy to tell you if Winky saw the holdup. See if Winky knows who did it."

Callie picked a leaf of lemon verbena and crushed it in the palm of her hand, sniffing at the fragrance of it. "None of the men around Mr. Hoag's store will take his word for it."

"Granted. But it would give us something to work on, wouldn't it?"

"I can try." Callie didn't sound very hopeful. "I tried to tell Tansy and Winky to get away from the Indian camp. But he was still there when the men rode in."

"That's another reason why I am inclined to think that Winky did not rob the stage," said Mr. Patch. "If he had committed that crime, I am sure Winky would have evacuated these parts that afternoon. It stands to reason."

"Yes, it does."

"See what you can do with Tansy, California. We have very little time."

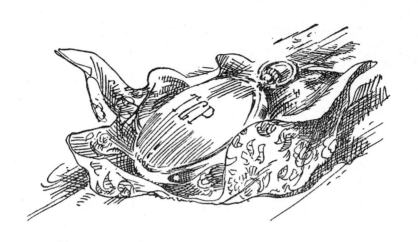

XIV TANSY'S
COOKING BASKET

Callie was waiting for her mother at the front gate when Ma and Sma' John came home from the quilting.

"Could I go into town, Ma, to see Tansy?" Callie hurried on when she saw her mother's frown. "It's still light, Ma. I promise to be back by dark. Mr. Patch thinks that Winky might have seen the holdup. He was over on the Bootjack trail that afternoon. Maybe he saw who did it. I'm not sure I can make Tansy understand, but Mr. Patch wants me to try."

Ma was shaking her head as she walked up the

garden, with Sma' John stumbling with tiredness beside her. "Tansy's smarter than we think," Ma was saying. "But I'm not sure I want you mixed up in this, Callie. It's going to be mighty ugly before we're through."

Callie followed her mother into the house. "But don't you see that's why I have to try? Please, Ma? If we can find out who did it—we have to find out who did it—it's the only way we'll get Winky out of jail."

Ma, standing in the middle of the kitchen floor, untied her bonnet, her eyes on Callie's pleading face. "I don't know——" she began. Suddenly she nodded. "Go ahead, Callie. If Pa were here he'd want us to do what we can. Take the brown betty I made this noon down to Winky. It's in the oven."

Ma wrapped a napkin around the pan of warm apple pudding, and Callie held it carefully all the way into town.

Callie didn't find Tansy at the jail. The old Indian woman was nowhere in sight.

Callie walked clear around the jail. She found the sheriff sitting in his chair on the shady side against the jail wall, whistling as he whittled. Callie remembered Andy's scornful words, "Tell it to the sheriff!"

"Hel-lo, Callie Dean. What you got there? Sompin' for a pore ole man tired of settin' here all day?"

"No, sir. It's a pudding for Winky, Mr. Sheriff. Ma sent it."

"Well, you keep it where I can't get a good whiff

of it, then. I'm almost ready to rob a stage myself, just to get some of the good home cookin' Winky gets."

The dimple in Callie's chin began to flicker. "That's because Ma and the rest of these women don't think he did it, sir."

The sheriff considered this. "Mebbe he did, an' mebbe he didn't. But we got to prove it, this way or that."

"Mr. Diamond said Joe Scald——"

"I know all about that. But Joe wasn't in no fix to tell whether what he saw was red, white, or blue." The sheriff laughed at his little joke.

"Mr. Hoag and Mr. Turnbeck say they aren't going to wait much longer before they haul Winky out of jail."

The sheriff chuckled. "Don't you fret, Callie." He put his jackknife back in his pocket. "These loud-mouths will wait as long as I say so. There hasn't been any excitement around here for a bit, so they have to blow off some steam. But when it comes to movin' Winky, I'm the law."

But as Callie started around the jail to find Tansy, she was wondering if the law and one man could stop ten or twelve men determined to take the law in their own hands.

She found Tansy seated below the jail window, one leg curled under her, the other straight out. Tansy was eating acorn mush from a small tan and black cooking basket. She dipped her curved fingers into the sticky paste and sucked them off with smacking lips.

"Hello, Tansy." Callie dropped down on the dry grass beside the old squaw and leaned back against the wall of the jail.

"'Allo." Tansy offered Callie some of her mush. Callie dipped her fingers in and sucked them off. She didn't care much for acorn mush. It tasted gluey and unsalted. But it was the best Tansy had and Callie accepted it.

She handed the apple pudding to Tansy. "It's for Winky. Ma sent it." She lifted a corner of the fringed napkin to show Tansy the still-warm crust of crumbs and brown sugar.

Tansy's face crinkled up with pleasure. She scooped out a generous handful from the pan and licked it up. She rolled her eyes and patted her tummy as Sma' John might have done. Callie laughed. Tansy put the napkin back on top of the pudding and placed the pan carefully beside the stone wall.

Callie sat quietly beside her, staring out across the creek to the hillside beyond. The sun was down behind the hills, leaving a golden light on the top of Bootjack Mountain. The shadows were long across the canyon. A chorus of frogs down by the creek sounded like a thousand creaking doors. A lone dog trotted by on business of his own, looking neither to right nor to left. A companionable silence had settled down on the two of them.

Callie wasn't sure how to begin what she had to say. "Listen, Tansy."

The old woman pulled her gaze from the gold-green trees and looked at Callie.

Callie lowered her voice. "Can anybody hear us here?"

"Winky hear." Tansy jerked her head at the barred window overhead.

"That's all right. It's about Winky. How about the sheriff? Is he close enough?"

"He go eat."

"All right. Now. We have to find out who robbed that stage, Tansy—fast! Those men aren't going to wait much longer. They'll haul Winky out of there, first thing you know. Look, Tansy. You ask him if he saw the man who did it? Ask Winky if he knows, huh?"

The old woman's face was a blank mask. "Winky no see."

"Now listen, Tansy. I saw Winky go over the Boot-jack trail that day. In plenty of time to catch the stage. No—wait, Tansy. Don't get uppity. If Winky went all the way over that hill, he might have seen the stage go by. Did he? He might have even seen the holdup."

The old woman began humming one of her slow, monotonous songs. She had turned her shoulder to Callie. She had turned her eyes to the sunlit hills.

Callie squirmed with impatience. "Tansy, talk to Winky," she coaxed. "Ask him if he saw the stage. Ask him if he knows who it was who held it up. If we knew that, we could help Winky. We could get him out of jail."

Tansy put her head back against the warm stones of the jail and closed her eyes. The song droned on, a low rumble from somewhere deep in the shapeless bundle that was Tansy Loosefoot.

"Oh, Tansy!" groaned Callie. "Pay attention. Don't you want to get Winky out of jail? I'm trying to help. Find out from Winky if he saw who did it."

Tansy got slowly to her feet, picking up the napkin from the apple pudding as she stood up. She scooped up the last of the mush from the basket and sucked it from her fingers. She dug deep in the pocket of her Mother Hubbard dress and brought out something hidden in her hand. She slid it into the fringed napkin, wrapping it tight. She put this small bundle in the bottom of the mush basket.

Callie got to her feet as the sheriff and Mr. Hoag came out of the eating place across the way.

Tansy shoved the small basket into Callie's hands. "You take," she said urgently. "You keep."

Callie took the basket. She turned away as the old woman picked up the apple pudding and headed around the jail to wait for the sheriff at the iron door.

As the two men crossed the street, the sheriff was saying, "I ain't got anybody's word but yours that Winky went over that way. It don't make sense for an Indian to hold up the stage. The minute he tried to cash that gold, he'd stick his head in a noose. It'd be a dead giveaway."

"You don't think Winky's smart enough?" Mr. Hoag's high whine was scornful. "He's smart enough to get away with things in my store whenever he feels like it."

"I don't know," answered the sheriff. "The Loose-foots never gave us any trouble before. Maybe you just got things buried away in that store where you can't find 'em. You got things in there you haven't seen for years. You don't know the half of what you got in that mumble-jumble." The sheriff laughed at his little joke.

Mr. Hoag was angry. "I tell you that whole kit an' caboodle are born thieves. An' Winky had plenty of time to cross that mountain. Here's Callie now. She saw him. You tell the sheriff, Callie, how you saw Winky go up the Bootjack trail, Friday after-noon, in plenty of time to hold up the stage."

Callie smiled at the sheriff. She was clutching the mush basket, holding the hard lump in the bottom of it with her thumb. "You're just like my father, Mr. Sheriff." She turned to Mr. Hoag. "The sheriff and Pa both know the Loosefoots are honest. Pa said he could always depend on Winky. I think the sheriff feels the same way."

"Now, Callie!" sputtered Mr. Hoag.

"I have to hurry," said Callie. "I promised Ma I'd be home by dark."

"Well, first you tell the sheriff how you saw Winky take off for Bootjack that very afternoon," urged Mr. Hoag.

Callie looked puzzled. "Let's see. Was that the last day of school?"

The sheriff chuckled. "Hear you got into trouble, Callie, slingin' mud. Sure carried me back. I betcha Luke taught you that trick. He mud balled that Appaloosy mare I had. Caught her on the rump. She took me halfway to Bootjack, jumpin' like a jack rabbit, before I calmed her down. Time I got back in town I never could locate Luke high nor low. I sure woulda tanned him good."

Callie flushed. "I have to get back home," she said uncomfortably. "It'll be dark directly."

She was gone before Mr. Hoag could put out his hand to stop her. "But Callie——" she heard him sputter behind her.

Callie waited until she was well out of town before she looked in the Indian basket. As she unfolded the napkin something heavy rolled out of it. Callie stared at it with stricken eyes.

It was Mr. Patch's watch, his grandfather's watch. It was a watch that could tell the time of day, the day of the week, and the month of the year.

It was, also—and no one knew this better than Callie—a watch that could easily tell the end of old Tansy's son, Winky Loosefoot.

XV MR. PATCH'S GOLD WATCH

Callie slid the heavy gold watch into the pocket of her dress. All the way home her mind was in a whirl. Had she been wrong about Winky? About Tansy? Where had Tansy found the watch? Had Winky given it to her? Where was the rest of the gold?

Callie didn't know what she should do with the watch, now she had it. Should she turn it over to the sheriff? Wouldn't he arrest Tansy as soon as he knew she had given the watch to Callie? What else could he do? Even if she believed Callie when she told him Winky didn't do it, could he hold out against all those men who chose to believe that

Winky did? If they heard that Tansy had given Callie the watch, wouldn't that settle it once and for all? Callie was pretty sure it would.

They'd know then that somehow the Indians were mixed up with the holdup, whether or not Winky had held up the stage.

Callie said nothing to Ma about the watch when she told her about her talk with Tansy. She had made up her mind. She had decided that she was not going to tell anybody about the watch that was weighing like lead in her pocket.

"I couldn't get anything out of Tansy," she told Ma.

"Tansy understands more than she's willing to let on," answered Ma as she smoothed the finely woven sides of the basket Tansy had given Callie. "It's a real nice basket."

Callie sighed. "Well, I'd rather she'd told me whether Winky knows about the holdup. I talked and talked, but she didn't say a word."

"She's afraid, poor thing. Maybe she will, after she has talked to Winky."

But Tansy didn't need to tell anybody anything. In the morning Winky Loosefoot was gone from the jail. During the night two men had bound and gagged the sheriff, taken his keys, and opened the inner jail door. They had an extra horse for Winky. The sheriff had heard the three of them ride away.

"I didn't see either one of them," he told the men who cut him loose. "It was pitch dark."

"Couldn't you tell by their talk?"

"It was so hot in that jail you couldn't spit. I left the door open. They caught me asleep an' never said a word. First thing I knew they had me gagged and trussed. They took my keys an' tried 'em all until they got the one that fit."

When Callie came down to the store that morning and heard the news, every bit of empty space was full of angry men.

"How soon we goin' to start chasin' after Winky?" shouted one of them.

"Where's Joe Sparrow? He can track 'em for us."

"Three horses. The tracks are plain. They headed up past Sawmill Mountain."

Andy pushed his way in beside Callie. "What are you doing down here, Bean Pole? If you got to get something, get it quick and get out."

"Same thing you are. Finding out what they're up to."

Mr. Hoag's eyes were narrow slits when he saw Callie. He thrust his sticky, unshaven face across the counter. The peppermint stick waggled between his lips. "What were you doin', Callie Dean, I'd like to know, over at the jail last evenin'? Just tell me that. I saw you sittin' over there hand an' glove with old Tansy."

A hard silence fell. The men turned to stare at Callie.

"You won't say you saw Winky go over the hill to Bootjack the day he robbed the stage, an' now, when those varmints were about to clear out, you was over at the jail. Whose side are you Deans on in this deal?"

"I——" began Callie, her eyes snapping.

"She took old Tansy some food for Winky is all," drawled Andy. "My mother did, too. Any crime in that?"

"You two clear out of here," ordered Mr. Hoag angrily.

"We have as much right——" began Callie.

"Come on, String Bean, and shut up." Andy pushed her ahead of him to the door. "You talk too much." He jumped down the steps and started off, leaving Callie on the porch of the store.

"Where you going?" Callie asked.

"It's none of your business, Bean Pole, but Mr. Patch and I are going up the mountain. I got to go home and get my shoes."

Callie ran to catch up with Andy's long strides. "Where up the mountain are you two going?"

Andy's grin was provoking. "Don't you wish you knew?"

He walked off down the street singing as he went. It was a song the men of the Gold Rush had brought with them by wagon or sail, to the tune of "Yankee Doodle."

"Gold is got in pan and pot,
Soup tureen and ladle,
Basket, birdcage and what not,
Even to a cradle—

133

Choose your able-bodied men,
All whose arms are brawny,
Give them picks and spades and then
Off for Californy!"

Callie was furious. "You can't go without me. You took me before. You couldn't have talked with Tansy if you hadn't."

"You go on home and wash the dishes," Andy called back. "This isn't a girl's business." He strode off down the boardwalk, his bare feet slapping against the planks.

Callie stood in the dusty road biting her lip. She couldn't bear to have the two of them go off without her.

When Andy reached the corner of the blacksmith shop, Callie picked up her skirts and ran after him. The heavy watch banged against her leg as she ran.

Andy turned around, glowering. "Who said you could tag along? Thought I told you to go on home."

"You tell Mr. Patch," she said breathlessly, "that I have something that he'd like to have very much. Something really and truly important!"

"Aw! You have not!"

"I have so!" Callie dug in her pocket for the gold watch. She held it out under Andy's nose. "There! That's what I have, Smarty Jensen!"

Andy's eyes were large and round. "Where'd you get it?"

Callie pushed the watch deep into her pocket.

She turned on her heel and Andy ran after her. His voice was low and urgent. "Callie Dean, you

want to get into real trouble? You want to get Winky hanged? Where did you get that watch?"

Callie swung her braids back over her shoulders. She made her knees push her skirts out in front of her in little puffs. She was humming a tuneless song like Tansy's. As Andy caught her arm, she smiled sweetly at him. "Don't you just *wish* you knew!"

Later in the morning Mr. Patch found Callie stirring clothes in the big soap kettle, over a slow fire, out under the apple trees. She was trying to keep the soap off her clothes. Ma had told her to keep stirring so the clothes wouldn't scorch.

"Don't stop stirring those clothes for a minute," Ma had said.

Callie glanced at the schoolmaster. She went on stirring with her long stick. "Ma's gone to the store with Sma' John. Things are so riled up over Winky I couldn't get what I went for this morning. Ma doesn't want me to go into town any more."

"That is the wiser course," said Mr. Patch. He sat down on an overturned tub. "Er—ah—California?"

"Yes, Mr. Patch?" Callie concentrated on the swirling clothes.

"Andy tells me—ah—he says—it's hard to believe, really——"

"What is, Mr. Patch?" Callie went on poking and stirring. The dimple in her chin was flickering, but she kept her eyes on the tubful of clothes.

"Andy tells me that you have my watch!" The words came out in a rush.

"Yes I have."

"You have it here?"

"No, sir. After I showed it to Andy this morning, I put it in a real safe place." She smiled at him. "I knew you wouldn't want anything to happen to it."

"Of course not. Oh, no!" Mr. Patch mopped his forehead with his folded handkerchief.

Callie went on stirring.

Mr. Patch leaned forward, his bony hands on the knees of his rusty black suit. He pushed the loose lock of hair from his forehead. "What consideration, California, what recompense do you require for that watch? I am prepared to pay——"

Callie was shocked. She stopped her stirring. "Why, Mr. Patch! I don't want money! I wouldn't think of taking *money* for your watch."

The long stick turned idly with the sluggish clothes. She scooped up a generous handful of soft soap from a bucket. She scraped it off her fingers and into the kettle with a chip.

"Then what do you want, California?" Mr. Patch slid his fingers in and out of his empty vest pocket. "No questions asked, for one thing? Is that it?"

Callie prodded the clothes with her stick. "Yes, sir." She looked at him, her jaw set. "And if you and Andy are going off to try and find Tansy or Winky, I want to go, too."

Mr. Patch pursed his lips. He shook his head. "I am afraid not. Anders and I are acting on pure hazard. We plan to go up to the Indian camp on Custer Creek. Anders will show me how to get there. We

137

are looking for evidence, California. This is not something in which a girl should be concerned."

Callie punched the clothes angrily. "So far I've been concerned in it as much as anybody." She drew a deep breath. "You can't have the watch then." Her voice was stubborn. "Not unless you let me go."

Mr. Patch got up. "I'm sure the watch is quite safe with you, California. Safer, I suspect, than it would be with me. Everybody in town knows I lost that watch in the holdup. If these men in Hardpan should see me with it, I would have some explaining to do." He started for the gate. "I'll leave the watch in your hands for the time being, California. I know you will take good care of it."

Callie was too disappointed and angry to answer him.

Mr. Patch looked at her downcast face. "We are taking a shovel and an ax with us, California. The time for talking is past."

XVI "IT IS TOO
A GIRL'S BUSINESS!"

The longer Callie stirred, after Mr. Patch was gone,
the madder she got. "It is too a girl's business!" She
punched the words down into the soapy, boiling water. "As much as anybody's!"

Callie felt that what had happened to Winky, and
what might happen between now and tomorrow, was
everybody's business. She felt left out, with Andy going off with Mr. Patch. Up to now it had been Callie
who had talked with Tansy at the camporee and at
the jail. It was Callie who had cut down the rope.
It was Callie to whom Tansy had entrusted the

watch. Hadn't all of that been a girl's business? Up to now it had been Callie's business more than everybody's.

She looked up to see old Tansy flitting silently from one tree to another in the small orchard.

"My goodness, Tansy. What are you doing here? I thought you'd be a long way off by now. Why aren't you up in the mountains?"

Tansy sat down on the ground beside the soap bucket. She seemed to blend into the tree trunk behind her. She laid the empty apple-pudding pan beside her on the ground. She squinted at Callie, her face tucked and puckered with laughter.

"Did Winky get away safe?" whispered Callie.

"Winky all gone." The old woman laughed until her whole body shook. "Tom come. Take Winky long way."

So it was the Indians who had freed Winky. Good! Then Callie remembered the watch. Her voice was worried. "Where'd you get that watch, Tansy?"

Tansy shrugged. "Tansy find it in Winky's house."

Callie was sick at heart. "Oh, no!"

Tansy rolled over and hoisted herself to her feet. "Go now." She made a motion of putting food in her mouth. "Me muy malo. Pocito pan? Me muy malo."

"You'd better have some. You wait here, Tansy. I'll get you some." Callie found it hard to think or to plan after what Tansy had just told her.

Callie ran into the house. She put some bread and some stale biscuits in a meal sack. Recklessly she cut

140

off half the haunch of cooked meat hanging in the
screened safe. She was saying over and over the
shocking words, "In Winky's house! In Winky's
house!"

Tansy grunted her thanks when Callie gave her
the sack. She dug down in the front of her dress and
brought up a bundle wrapped in gray calico. It was
full of shelled piñon nuts, sweet and crisp. She
pressed the nuts into Callie's hands, slung the sack
of bread and meat over her shoulder, and turned to
go.

Callie held her back for a moment. Her last hope
of finding Winky innocent of the holdup was gone.
But she couldn't bear to have him tracked down and
caught. "Tansy, those men are going after Winky.
They mean to track him."

Tansy's laugh bubbled up from deep in her throat.
"Na. Men no track Winky. Tracks all gone bime by.
Bueno."

She half turned, stood for a moment beside the
fire, pushing her moccasined foot against the apple
pan. "Winky say," she said in a clear voice, "Jim
Turnbeck rob stage." She spat into the coals, and the
spit hissed and crackled. "Winky watch. Jim Turnbeck put gold in ground. Hide watch in Winky's
house. Gold under bent tree at Cold Spring." She
smiled into Callie's startled face as she turned away.

The next moment she was gone, lost in the orchard
trees.

Callie stood still in complete surprise. She had just
this minute got used to the idea that Winky was

guilty after all. Now it wasn't Winky. It was Jim Turnbeck. Jim Turnbeck!

She wasn't sure what she should do. Should she go to the sheriff with this astounding news? How could she be sure he would believe old Tansy? Pa would. But Pa wasn't here. None of the men at the store would. Those men were against the Indians. They'd say that Winky was the one who had buried the gold at Cold Spring.

She was sure they wouldn't believe her if she told them it was Jim Turnbeck. Callie had a hard time believing it herself. Except that it made sense. All the bits of the puzzle slipped into place. If Jim Turnbeck held up the stage, of course he would want the men to hang Winky. He wanted Winky's land, but he also needed someone hanged for the stage holdup. He had hidden Mr. Patch's gold watch in Winky's hut to prove the Indians were involved. He could never feel secure until someone had paid for the holdup.

Maybe Mr. Patch would know what she should do. But Mr. Patch and Andy were gone.

Callie made up her mind to go after them before she went to the sheriff.

She dragged the big wooden tub over close to the fire. She caught up the dripping clothes with the long stick and lifted them into it. She couldn't leave clothes over the fire. They'd burn. Ma would be mad enough about her going alone to the Indian camp as it was.

Callie ran down to the Jensen house. "I have a

message for Mr. Patch, Mrs. Jensen," she said breathlessly. "How long have he and Andy been gone?"

Mrs. Jensen looked with disapproval at Callie's flushed face and soap-spattered dress. "Half an hour iss gone, maybe."

Half an hour was a long head start. She'd never catch up with them this side of Custer Creek. But it didn't matter. She knew now that she had to find them, and the sooner the better.

Callie went back home again. She slapped together a huge sandwich of bread and meat. She put this and the biggest apple she could find in the root cellar in a bandana and tied the bundle to her belt. She poured herself a mug of buttermilk. She drank it fast, her eyes on the front gate. She knew she must get away before Ma and Sma' John came home. Ma would never be willing to let her go to the Indian camp alone, even if she knew what Callie's message was.

"This isn't a girl's business," she'd say. Girl's business indeed! This was what Mr. Patch and the sheriff and the Jensens and Ma had been waiting for. It was the only thing that would ever save Winky.

Before she set out Callie pulled one of Pa's old hats over her head. She put the piñon nuts Tansy had given her in a little pile on the kitchen table for Sma' John. She went out through the orchard, not wanting to meet Ma and the small boy on the road.

She looked back from the hill above the sawmill. She could see men and horses milling around on the street in front of the store. She was glad they hadn't

started off tracking Winky. But if the tracks led up toward the Indian camp, she'd have to make good time to get there before the men could. She'd take the short cut Andy had shown her the day they picked berries on the sawmill hill.

Callie had never climbed so fast as she did that morning. It seemed forever before she reached the top of the slope looking down into Custer Creek. Catching up her skirts she ran down the trail to the Indian camp.

When she came out of the trees into the meadow, neither Mr. Patch nor Andy was in sight. The meadow, brown-green and fringed with the flame of wind poppies, drowsed peacefully in the morning sun. There were no horses grazing, no fires burning. A warm wind blew against Callie's flushed face, lifting the curls from her damp forehead. For a moment she was full of panic because she didn't know where else to look for Mr. Patch.

Then she caught a movement in one of the brush huts. She hurried over, out of breath, to face Andy coming out of the hut.

Andy wasn't pleased to see her. "What business have you got coming up here, Callie Dean?"

"I have a message for Mr. Patch."

"I bet you haven't!" He turned as Mr. Patch came over from one of the other huts. "She says she has a message."

"A message, California?"

"Yes, sir," she answered, turning her back on Andy. She took a deep breath. "It's from Tansy. Winky told her it was Jim Turnbeck who robbed the stage. He watched Jim Turnbeck bury the gold at Cold Spring, under a bent tree."

Andy whistled. "Well, good for you, String Bean!"

"Well! Well! But what do you make of this, California?" Mr. Patch held out a small, heavy cone of metal.

"Why, that's gold!" said Callie. "The way they melt it down at the smelter. Where did you find it?"

"Here. In one of the Indian huts. Winky's, I suspect. Buried not too deep, and the ground recently dug up."

"But Tansy said——"

"I am quite convinced she is right. Jim Turnbeck must have planted this gold here for the men to find."

"To prove Winky did it?"

"That is my conclusion. Simple-minded, isn't it? But it would be damaging evidence to simple-minded men. We have been checking to be certain that Winky's hut was the only place where anything was buried. The other huts do not seem to have been disturbed."

"Tansy said Jim Turnbeck hid your watch in Winky's house. She found it there, but she must have missed the gold."

"Tsk! Tsk! Tsk! Villainy compounded! Jim Turnbeck probably found the watch gone and planted this cone of gold in its place. He'd want to make certain that there was something here for the men to find."

"They might be here pretty soon," said Callie.

146

"Yes," answered Mr. Patch. "We must not be caught in here. We'll let Jim Turnbeck lead them to this dug-up spot. My only regret is for not seeing his face when he discovers his planted evidence is gone. Can you show us the way to Cold Spring, Anders?"

"If we climb the hill above here, we can cut across the slash," said Andy. "Or we can go back to the sawmill and take the trail from there."

"By all means let us climb from here. We should not risk meeting the hunt, should we? Take the shovel, Anders. I shall carry the ax. I rather think we shall have to dig deeper this time for gold."

Andy went back to get his shovel.

"Well, California, I can see nothing for it but to let you accompany us to Cold Spring."

Callie grinned.

"Why does she have to tag along?" growled Andy.

"Fi, Anders! Where would we be without this redoubtable Amazon? Certainly not headed for Cold Spring and buried treasure. It would not do for us to abandon Callie for the posse to find between here and Hardpan. Everybody get a good drink of water. I'll fill my leathern bottle at the spring."

The noon sun beat down upon them as they climbed up the steep slope above the meadow.

"Whew!" whistled Mr. Patch, pausing for breath. "I can not keep up the pace you set us, Anders."

Callie was glad he was with them. She knew how hard it was to keep up with Andy, and how cross he could get when she didn't.

"Once we are out of sight of this camp," said Mr.

Patch, "we won't have to travel so fast. Jim Turnbeck will be glad to lead the men in here to Custer Creek, but he will keep them a long way from that bent tree at Cold Spring."

"Well, I'd better get there—and get home again," said Callie. "My mother doesn't know where I am."

Mr. Patch shouldered his ax. "That's a horse of a different color. 'Lay on, Macduff!' "

It was rough going, around and over stumps and rocks and the fallen trees left by the lumbering. Mr. Patch puffed along after Andy. Callie scrambled after both of them. They reached the end of the cut-over land and faced a long, steep slope of dry grass. A clear trail was marked where the ripe grass had been broken and trampled. The bent straw made a silver streak across the gold of the standing grass.

"Somebody's been over this way," Andy pointed out. "Not too long ago. Three horses."

"Then it was Winky," said Callie. "Tom Loosefoot and, I guess, another Indian were the ones who took him out of the jail." She was frowning at the tracks. "It would be awfully easy to track them, wouldn't it?"

Andy had shaded his eyes against the pale glare of the sky. "Look!" He pointed far below to where a puff of smoke billowed up and melted away in the bright air. Another puff became a steady column of smoke.

"What does that mean, Anders?" asked Mr. Patch sharply.

"Somebody's fired the grass, sir. With the wind in this direction, it's bound to come this way."

"Why would anybody want to set a fire?" asked Callie.

"It's a good way to cover tracks," answered Mr. Patch.

Callie remembered Tansy's words, "Tracks all gone bime by."

"How can we get out of here, Anders?" Mr. Patch's voice sounded worried. "This is no place to be caught by a grass fire. It will sweep up these slopes like a blast from a smelter."

"I'm not sure we can," said Andy, testing the wind on a wet finger. "The wind's this way, and the fire will follow the wind."

Callie had seen grass fires on the hills behind Hardpan. She knew how fiercely they burned and how fast they ran. Her eyes were frightened as she watched the widening columns of smoke.

"Come on!" urged Mr. Patch. "We have no time to lose if we expect to outrun that fire."

XVII "A WORLD OF FLICKERING FLAME"

"We must keep ahead of the fire," said Mr. Patch. "If we swing over to the left, out of this draw, it may bypass us."

They started climbing the steep slope. There were few bushes on this side of the mountain, but the wild grass was as slippery as glass. Callie tried her best to dig in. She slipped and slithered, until it seemed like a nightmare where she stayed rooted in one spot or slipped back two steps for one. The smoke below them had spread until it shut off all of Hardpan gulch.

Mr. Patch stopped, out of breath. "It does not look salubrious," he panted. "It's coming too fast. I'm not sure we are going to get away from it, Anders."

"No, sir. I'm looking for an open spot, mostly grass.

Mr. Patch shaded his eyes to look down at the spreading smoke below. "You mean to let it burn right over us, Anders?"

"Around us, sir, if the grass isn't too high. Grass fires burn hot, but the edge is just a fringe of flame. We need a place where there's no brush or down timber to catch fire. If we work fast, we can make a firebreak. Then the fire will burn around us."

"Very well, Anders, if that is the best we can hope for. We shall let you pick a good spot for us."

"Come on, Callie!" growled Andy.

The smoke had covered the eastern sky, mushrooming into a great white thunderhead. It was spreading up the mountain with the freshening wind. The sunlight dimmed, until the sun became a small, round, blood-red ball behind the rolls of smoke.

Callie's breath was short and her lungs ached as she tried to keep up with the others. Her heart was pounding in her chest.

"'S matter with you anyway?" grumbled Andy. "Can't you keep up? We'll be cooked for sure if you don't hustle."

"I'm—trying—to." Callie's voice came between painful gulps. She stepped on her skirt and stumbled, sliding down to her knees.

Mr. Patch caught her under one arm. "Take her other arm, Anders. There now, up you go!"

Callie laughed shakily as they pushed and shoved her up the mountain over the slippery grass. The smell of smoke was getting stronger.

They came out onto a flat, fairly level stretch of grass. The rest of the slopes below had disappeared in a blue haze.

"This is as good as we're likely to find," said Andy. "Anyway, we haven't time to hunt up anything better. The grass is short, and there's enough wind to draw off the worst of the smoke."

"Break the soil ahead of me with the ax, Anders," said Mr. Patch, "into chunks. I shall shovel them over with the grass on the underside. That should make a firebreak. We must get it wide enough so that the fire will not jump across."

Andy began chopping down into the hard soil with his ax. Mr. Patch followed him, spading up the loosened chunks of sod and turning the grass under. Callie came behind them trampling and stamping the last wisps of grass into the ground. They worked across the lower end and up the sides of the level stretch, digging up and turning over a brown ribbon of safety to hold off the flames.

The smoke was thick now. They couldn't tell how close the fire was. The air was stifling. Heat and smoke poured up the canyon until all of them choked and strangled.

"Soak your handkerchiefs in the water from my leathern bottle," said Mr. Patch. His shovel rang against a rock and he grunted. He stopped long enough to pour water on his handkerchief, tying it around his nose and mouth.

Callie untied her bandana. She laid the sandwich and apple in the shade of a rock. It was much easier to breathe when she had wet the bandana and tied it around her face.

The grim business of digging up and trampling down the ground went on. Andy beat out the first glowing spark that landed on Callie's dress with his bare hands.

Mr. Patch stripped off his coat. He lifted the edge of his handkerchief to talk. "Take yours off, too, Anders. Here, Callie, take this, and you two use the coats to beat out any spot fires that start inside the firebreak."

Callie's eyes were streaming as she took the coat. Andy took off his own coat. He and Callie flailed at the burning grass underfoot. Callie had shoved her braids up under Pa's old hat. She was thankful she had brought it along, for it protected her hair from the burning leaves and sparks raining down upon them. Small glowing embers burned her dress or hands before she could brush them off. Tiny round holes were burnt in her dress before she noticed where the live sparks had lit.

A cloud of winged gnats flew against her face and stuck to her wet skin. Grasshoppers blundered into her and went clicking and whirring on. A small red fox streaked by to dive into a hole higher up. Lower down the canyon deer fled by like gray ghosts in the smoke.

Now they could hear the crackling of the flames. Mr. Patch went calmly on with his spading. Andy and Callie beat out sparks that set fire to the grass in their small island behind the widening firebreak.

At one point Mr. Patch leaned heavily on his shovel for a moment's rest. He looked at the firebreak and then down into the smoke below.

"'And naught twixt heaven and earth save a world of flickering flame,'" he quoted.

Callie laughed shakily at anybody taking time out to quote anything with a mountain of fire ready to engulf them.

The slim brown ribbon of spaded earth ran around three sides of them. When the time came they could

all trample out the flames at the upper end, if the fire
should come back that way.

"Here she comes!" shouted Andy.

Through the smoke they could see the flames. They
could hear the roaring and crackling. Small bushes
below them flared up and burned fiercely. The line
of fire whooshed up the slope below them.

"Turn your face up, Callie," shouted Mr. Patch.
He poured water recklessly over her bandana. He
sloshed some of it on the handkerchief over his own
face, before he handed the bottle to Andy.

Callie stamped out a flaming leaf that landed at
her feet.

"Put the coats over our heads!" commanded Mr.

Patch. They crouched together. Andy and Mr. Patch held the two coats closely about their heads and faces.

The fire raged up the hill. It curled along the edge of the firebreak and died. On both sides of them it crackled on up the canyon. There was a flare of searing heat as the fire passed. They could hear the flames snapping in the gully above them and the roar as the thick bushes caught and blazed.

Their own island of grass was blotched and blackened with burned spots. The choking smoke had thinned until they could see the burned slopes below them.

The fire had run around them, and was gone.

"You picked an excellent spot, Anders," Mr. Patch said thickly through his handkerchief, "to fight through our own private inferno."

"Yes, sir."

"I do not think we need to worry further about Winky's tracks." He pulled the blackened handkerchief from his face. "They are quite gone now, and they nearly took us with them." He heaved a long sigh. "My! My! I could do with a spot of tea."

"I have a sandwich," said Callie, "and an apple. They are covered with ash, but not too bad."

"Bless my soul!" Mr. Patch eyed her blackened face, her burned and bedraggled dress. "Such a disreputable young person, California! You continue to amaze me."

"Yes, sir."

Mr. Patch cut the mammoth sandwich into three

equal portions. "How fortunate for us that your idea of a sandwich was such a substantial one, California. Here, Anders, our despised companion has provided us with ambrosia fit for the gods. I hope you are duly grateful."

"Yes, sir." Andy bit down into the bread and meat.

Mr. Patch divided the apple before he put on his coat. The coat was burned in many places. He pulled it this way and that to look over the damage. His hands and wrists were black with grime. He grinned at Callie. "I take back my comment on your disrepute, California. How could such a pot call a kettle black?"

They climbed across the face of the scorched mountain. The burned bushes crumbled into ashes as they brushed by. They kicked up blackened ash with every step. It settled over them until their red-rimmed eyes looked out of black faces like holes cut in a mask.

By some freak of wind, the fire had stopped at the upper edge of the canyon. On the other side the standing timber looked cool and inviting. They hurried down through the trees, following an abandoned logging road.

It was the middle of the afternoon before they reached Cold Spring. Below them was a sloping grassy meadow with a small stream running through it, the icy water fed by a welling spring sunk in the side of the mountain. The meadow was ringed with pines, with thick underbrush of mountain lilac, toyon, and deer brush. Callie could smell the pungent odor of bear clover soaking up the sun. Above the spring there were wild roses, pink and fragrant, and the purple bonnets of bush lupin.

No wonder Winky loved this spot. And who, she was thinking, had a better right to it.

"Ah-hh-hh!" Mr. Patch gave a happy sigh. He mopped his face with his grimy handkerchief. "How does it go—the *Odyssey?*" He appealed to Callie who looked quite blank.

"Meadows of softest verdure purpled o'er
With violets; it was a scene to fill
A god from heaven with wonder and delight."

He looked at his soiled handkerchief with distaste. "I cannot bear to return this filthy rag to my pocket." He dropped it on a large flat rock pocked with deep holes where generations of Indian women had sat to grind their acorn meal. Andy dropped his beside it.

They all had long cold drinks of delicious water from the spring. While Mr. Patch and Andy went off to hunt for the bent tree, Callie had washed her hands and face and arms. They were red with heat burn. Her lips were cracked and blistered. Then she washed out the three handkerchiefs. When Mr. Patch and Andy came back, the washing was already drying in the hot sun.

The schoolmaster thanked her for his clean handkerchief. "You have more talents than I ever dreamed you possessed, California. I am convinced you could survive on a desert isle."

"Yes, sir."

"Anders and I have, alas! located three bent trees. Did Tansy give you any hint as to how much bent she meant?"

"No, sir."

"A thousand pities. My back feels that it has done its stint of spading for the day. Three trees! Under one of them lies treasure. Not under the last one, I sincerely hope. Now then, Anders, where shall we start?"

"Let's start with the farthest one," suggested Andy. "Maybe we can tell if the ground's been dug up. Besides, I think it's the one Jim Turnbeck would have picked. He wouldn't want it to be too close to the spring. Lots of people know this place. The Indians think this water is some kind of good medicine."

"Well argued, Anders. Bring your ax. Perhaps you can again loosen the soil as I dig." He groaned. "My back quails at the very thought of it. The labors of Sisyphus could not have been more burdensome!"

They made their way across to the farthest bent tree. The ground under the tree looked smooth and unbroken beneath a thick layer of pine needles. They were about to leave, to search under another tree, when Callie stooped down and picked up something from under the woods trash. She held it out to Mr. Patch.

"Well! Well! Well!" exclaimed Mr. Patch, leaning on his shovel.

"What is it?" asked Andy.

"A clue!" answered Mr. Patch. "A veritable clue!"

Callie was brushing small twigs and leaves from a stick of peppermint candy.

XVIII   THE GOLD AT
COLD SPRING

"Mr. Hoag!" said Andy.

"Of course." Mr. Patch was nodding his head. "We should have thought of it before. Jim Turnbeck alone could never have carried a heavy express box all this way from the Bootjack Hill. He would have to have some help. Mr. Hoag is the very man for it."

"That's why Mr. Hoag was so anxious to get Callie to say she'd seen Winky go up the Bootjack trail," suggested Andy.

"He wanted Winky out of the way," said Callie.

They started to dig beneath the tree. The topsoil

had been well trampled down. Once this was dug up, the ground was soft. It had been spaded not too long ago. Andy and Mr. Patch took turns and the shovel fairly flew.

At last they came upon a stout, brass-bound express box. Mr. Patch pried up the lid. The box was packed with small cones of dull gold.

"Well, there it is," said Mr. Patch. "What luck to find it under the first tree."

"And look!" said Callie. "Stuffed down beside the gold."

Mr. Patch pulled out from the side of the box a pair of Indian moccasins with pink porcupine quills embroidering the toes of them.

Tucked up against the lid of the box was a small canvas sack with a drawstring. Mr. Patch unfastened the string and poured out into the lid of the express box some gold and silver money, two small sacks of gold dust, a handful of gold nuggets, several stick-pins, and a signet ring.

He stuffed it all back into the sack and handed it to Callie. "May I ask you to carry this, California? Andy and I have the ax and the shovel. We'll take this loot to the sheriff. It will be convincing proof of our story."

He spit on his hands, groaned, and reached for the shovel. "Now, if my back can stand it, we must bury the gold again."

"We can't just leave all this gold here!" Callie's voice was shrill with disappointment. "We have to take it with us."

"No, California, we cannot do it. Even in relays, I doubt if we could. We could never get anything as heavy as that box to the top of the mountain and down to Hardpan. Gold is not only the root of all evil, it is as heavy as sin. No, after we cover our tracks, we shall send the sheriff in here to make this find. We will tell him what we know. We will let him trick Jim Turnbeck into giving himself away. My guess is that both those scoundrels will be in here tonight. They know by now that the planted gold is gone from Winky's hut. They know that the Indians would never have gone back to the camporee once they got Winky free. They realize that somebody is on to their schemes and tricks. They will want to get this gold away to a safer place."

Callie still looked unhappy.

"If we took this box into town ourselves, California," Mr. Patch went on, "those men might claim we had dug it up from Winky's hut."

Callie could see that.

"We have only Tansy's word that it was Jim Turnbeck who robbed the stage. And a piece of peppermint to tell us that Mr. Hoag was here where the gold was buried. But if the sheriff sees those two men come in here to remove this gold, no one will need any further proof."

It took them a long time to fill in the hole. Mr. Patch insisted on gathering up every bit of dirt and tramping down the surface of the ground firm and hard. They scattered pine needles over the ground until it looked like the rest of the forest floor.

The sun was low above the western hills by the time they finished. Mr. Patch shouldered the shovel and started up the trail. He gave them no time to rest. "We must get back," he panted. "We need to notify the sheriff. Those two rascals know by now that the gold planted in the Indian hut is gone. They will be in here in short order to remove this box. We would not have Tansy this time to tell us where they dispose of it."

They found the sheriff saddling his horse in front of the jail. "Where've you been, Callie Dean?" he shouted. "Your ma's half crazy. I've been scouring the country. I was just about to go over and get your pa and the boys."

Callie shrank back behind Mr. Patch as she watched people begin to gather.

"Just a minute, Sheriff," said Mr. Patch. "I must have a word with you. May we retire to your office, sir?" Office was a real fancy name for the jail, Callie was thinking.

"If that tomboy was my young one——" the sheriff was muttering, glaring at Callie.

Once inside the jail, and the door shut against the curious crowd, Mr. Patch told the sheriff about the gold planted in the Indian hut.

"Yeah," said the sheriff. "We went in there on a wild-goose chase. Dug up the whole floor of Winky's hut. Never found a blessed thing. By the time we got done, the backhill was afire. There weren't any use tryin' to follow tracks after that."

"Those were just the conclusions at which we arrived," said Mr. Patch. "Now tell the sheriff, California, about Winky seeing the holdup and what Tansy told you about Jim Turnbeck."

"Jim Turnbeck!"

"Tansy told me that Winky followed the bandit," said Callie. "He saw it was Jim Turnbeck. He watched him bury the gold under a bent tree at Cold Spring."

Andy spoke up. "It's the tree seventy paces due north from the spring."

Callie thought that was smart of Andy. She hadn't thought of pacing it off.

"We found it there," Mr. Patch told the sheriff, "after Tansy told us where to look. We buried it again. We could not have brought it down. I am not man enough for that. Besides we felt reasonably certain these men here would have said that it was Winky who had buried it."

"They were bound and determined it was Winky," said the sheriff.

"Callie has the small sack of money," Mr. Patch went on. "We brought it back to show you." He told the sheriff about the peppermint stick.

Callie unwrapped her bandana to show it to the sheriff. "Do you need this piece of candy, sir, for evidence or something?"

The sheriff squinted down at the stick of peppermint. "No, sis, we'll catch those hombres redhanded."

Callie broke the stick in two, measured the pieces, and handed Andy the larger of the two.

"Well—er—thanks," he muttered.

"I suggest that you get over to Cold Spring as soon as possible," Mr. Patch told the sheriff. "There's plenty of cover. I think they will go back there to-night to remove their ill-gotten gains."

The sheriff hurried off to get some deputies and a pack horse to bring back the gold.

"I will go home with you, Callie," offered Mr. Patch. "We have some explaining to do."

Ma came flying down to the gate to meet them. She was so glad to see Callie all she said was, "Cal-lie! Callie! I've been so frightened!"

"California hunted us up to tell us where the gold was buried, Mrs. Dean," said Mr. Patch. "Tansy came here after Andy and I were gone."

"You should have let me know, Callie. And when the fire started I had no notion where you were."

"I know, Ma. I didn't think I'd be gone so long." No use telling Ma they were in the path of the fire. She'd see the burned places in Callie's clothes soon enough.

"Come in and have supper, all of you," said Ma.

"I'd better go home first," answered Andy. "I bet my mother's mad."

Sma' John put his arms around Callie's knees. "Ma cry," he told her. "Sma' John cry. Callie all lost. Eva-body cry." He caught her hand and pulled her into the kitchen. On the table there were two little piles of piñon nuts.

Callie hugged the little boy. She buried her face in his neck with a snuffle and snort that delighted him.

"Callie left those nuts for Sma' John, silly," she told him.

Sma' John wiggled out of her arms. He pushed one of the piles over to Callie's side of the table. "One-for-you-an'-one-for-me!" he chanted, his blue eyes shining just above the table top.

Callie went up to change her clothes, while Mr. Patch went out to the pump to wash off the soot and grime.

When Callie came back downstairs, she had Mr. Patch's gold watch in her hand. "You let me go with you, sir," she said, the dimple flickering in her chin. "So now I'll give this back."

Mr. Patch took the watch in his hands very gently. He put it to his ear. "Why, California! You've kept it wound!"

"Yes, sir."

"It's good to get it back. Now I can go off in peace to work in the woods. I'm going to ask them to hire Tom and Winky Loosefoot as sawyers. Your Pa and I will see that Winky gets back his land at Cold Spring. It may take some time, if Jim Turnbeck has filed on it. I doubt if he has. I think he has been bluffing. I think we can file on it for Winky."

Andy came back to have supper with them.

"Was your ma mad?" asked Callie.

"Right at first, she was. When she saw the burned holes in my coat what she said was 'First iss mud—und now holes!'"

Callie's cheeks were hot.

Mr. Patch eased himself down in a chair at the

table. "Ooo-oo! I ache in every bone. I do not have the proper frame for digging."

The fire-fighters were starved. For some time nobody said much of anything.

"We think Tansy set the fire," Mr. Patch was saying when he had eaten his way through two platefuls of greens and beans, together with Ma's beaten biscuit and plenty of sweet butter. "We think it is probable because she told Callie that the tracks would be gone by-and-by."

Callie reached into the pocket of her dress and drew out the black obsidian skinning knife. She held it out to Andy. "You can have it, if you like," she said.

Andy was overcome. "Gee whiz, thanks! It's the best Indian knife I ever saw."

"It's sharp enough to cut through rope, anyway," said Callie.

Andy cleared his throat. "I'm going to get Willie Binks, and we'll build us a sod fort down by the creek. The sod would be soft to cut there."

"How do you cut sod?"

"Like we did for the grass fire. That's where I got the idea. Cut a square of sod with the ax and lift it out with a shovel. Then use the sods like 'dobes."

"Will you let the girls help?"

Andy paused for a long ten seconds. He looked down at the shining black knife in his hand. "Mebbe." He leaned across Sma' John and lowered his voice. "We will—if you'll show us how you sling mud balls."

"Sure," answered Callie, grinning back at him.

She'd show that Andy.

168